Prison Number XR6890

Yvonne Stewart-Williams[Butler]

W0009741

Prison Number XR6890

Published by
Chipmunkapublishing
United Kingdom

http://www.chipmunkapublishing.com

My Mental Health Story And Gateway to Normal Living
Blogs, Tweets & Facebook images and texts.

Follows on from my legendary EBooks of mental health lived experience journey:
1.   'Altered Perceptions'. - The beginnings.
2.   'Still on the Cusp of Madness'. - Ten years on.
3.   'Heathen Massive'. - Famous Individuals and me, including 'Gandalf.

Anyone can experience a mental health problem.

Sometimes it's the little things
you do that make a big difference.

Find out what you can do.

It's time to talk. It's time to change

Prison Number XR6890

Prison Number XR6890

Prison Number XR6890

Prison Number XR6890

Yvonne Stewart Williams Butler and LGBTory
shared LGBTory's photo.

LGBTory

Ready for Pride in London. MG

mum-careconcern.blogspot.co.uk

FRIDAY, 17 JUNE 2016

Desperate Help Needed!

I know that I am not alone to have been feeling especially sad about the recent Orlando occurrence, plus deeply sickened by Jo Cox's murder

I desperately need your support in the wake of these two tragedies, to help me to change Lambeth Council's... mind about their 31st March 2016 axing of their Hate Crimes strategy with the police.

Prison Number XR6890

Prison Number XR6890

MONDAY, 23 MAY 2016

My Manifesto

What do you think of my manifesto?

As your Norwood Conservative MP

I, Yvonne Stewart-Williams, am a Brixton based, Black lesbian, working class, single mother of a teenaged son.

I work full time for a London based Homelessness Charity, supporting mainly working class people with complex needs of addiction, Criminal Justice System and mental health issues.

In addition I am studying part-time for a Degree with the OU - Open University.

I am a Quaker. I am currently a Quaker Overseer responsible for pastoral care.

I am a Woman Freemason.

I volunteer at the Brixton Soup Kitchen.

I am a Stonewall School Role Model.

I am a Gay Rights Campaigner.

I am a Mental Health Campaigner. I aim to champion:

LGBT Rights,

Faith

Looked After, Fostered and Adopted children,

Addiction issues

Criminal Justice issues

Mental Health issues

Equality issues - more women MP's in parliament. And be sympathetic to:

Gay Men with Mental Health issues - establish a cross party partnership to discover ways to help and support gay men to be integrated within society, by taking surveys and creating groups to discuss issues that affect gay and bi males.

Estranged fathers - work to support equality and access to loving productive fathers to their children by revisiting the family court procedure.

Working Class white males - and will work to establish a commission to discover why White Males under achieve at school and are under-represented at University and remedy it. Contact

Text My Mobile Number: 07490 165136.

Email: y_p_stewart_williams@hotmail.com

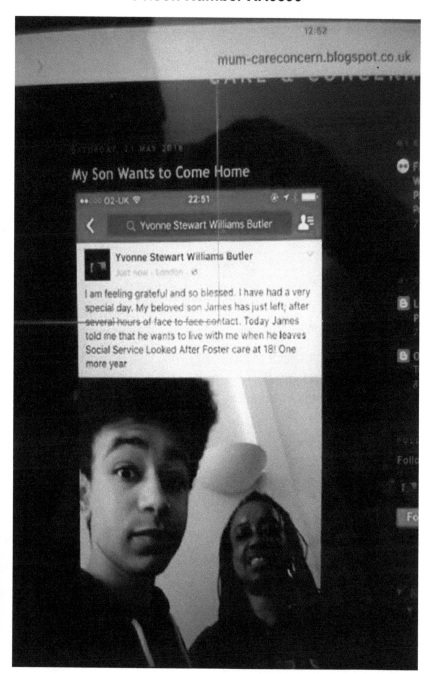

Prison Number XR6890

mum-careconcern.blogspot.co

WEDNESDAY, 18 MAY 2016

Huffington Post

Just to let you know that the Huffington Post has just published the article for Mental Health Awareness Week 2016 Interview which I did SANE:http://www.huffingtonpost.co.uk/heenali-patel/mental-health-care_b_10004070.html

FRIDAY, 13 MAY 2016

Friday 13th

Today I attended the funeral of my Conservative colleague Dr Enid May Parker.

Followed by lunch with a few Conservative WAG's, Women's Action Group colleagues.

Prison Number XR6890

St George's Day

This is a view today from the LSE (London School of Economics) window on my OU journal.

Today is also St George's Day and the 400th year of Arthur Shakespeare.

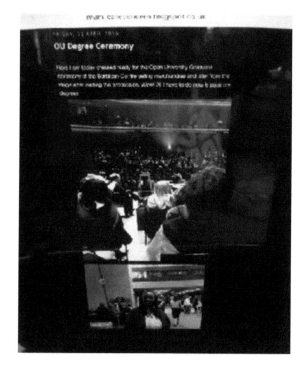

FRIDAY, 22 APRIL 2016

OU Degree Ceremony

Here I am today dressed ready for the Open University Graduate ceremony at the Barbican Centre setting mechanical and after from the magazine making the procession, about 26 I have to do now to pass my degree.

mum-careconcern.blogspot.co.uk

THURSDAY 14 APRIL 2016

Executive Meeting

Currently at 495 for a Dulwich & West Norwood Conservative
Association Executive Meeting.

Prison Number XR6890

Prison Number XR6890

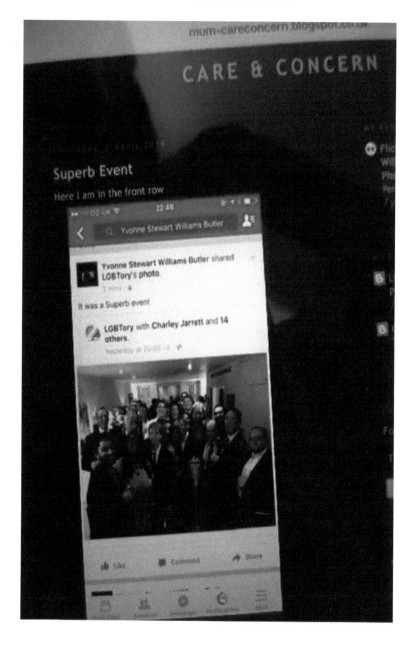

Prison Number XR6890

mum-careconcern.blogspot.co.uk

CARE & CONCERN

Me & Tony Waters

Me today with Tony Waters, just after my local Brixton & Streatham Quaker Friends Meeting for Worship

Prison Number XR6890

Prison Number XR6890

Prison Number XR6890

CARE & CONCERN

SATURDAY, 19 MARCH 2016

The Magic Flute

I was seated in the London Coliseum and enjoyed the Magic Flute opera by Mozart with the full spectacular display of the ENO English National Opera

Prison Number XR6890

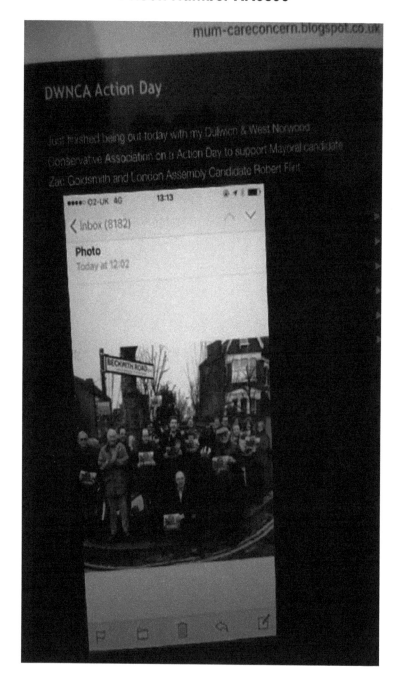

DWNCA Action Day

Just finished being out today with my Dulwich & West Norwood Conservative Association on a Action Day to support Mayoral candidate Zac Goldsmith and London Assembly Candidate Robert Flint

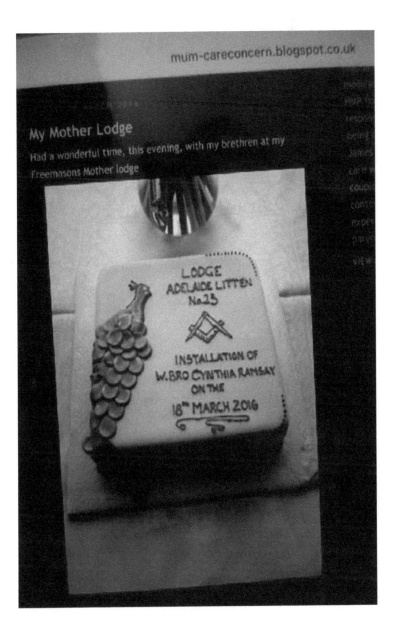

mum-careconcern.blogspot.co.uk

My Mother Lodge

Had a wonderful time, this evening, with my brethren at my
Freemasons Mother lodge

LODGE
ADELAIDE LITTEN
No.23

INSTALLATION OF
W.BRO CYNTHIA RAMSAY
ON THE

18ᵀᴴ MARCH 2016

mum-careconcern.blogspot.co.uk

Last Lesson at Ace of Clubs

Me today at my fourth bike maintenance course, tutored by Cycle
Training Uk at The Ace of Clubs Day Centre, in Clapham.

Next stop is a Brompton Basic Maintenance Day Course with Cycle
Training UK in Bermondsey on Saturday 11th June 2016

Prison Number XR6890

Today at Brixton Soup Kitchen, in Coldharbour Ward - Brixton with Solomon Smith, I am delighted to announce that I will begin volunteering for Brixton Soup Kitchen from 11am on Monday 21st March 2016

Prison Number XR6890

Prison Number XR6890

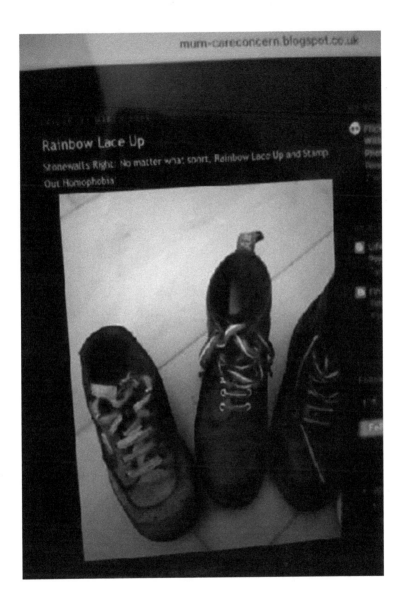

Rainbow Lace Up

Stonewalls Right: No matter what sport, Rainbow Lace Up and Stamp Out Homophobia

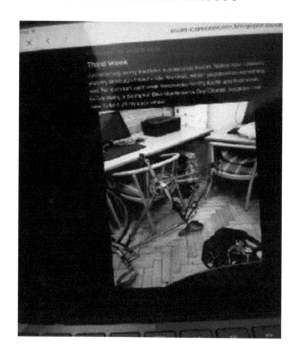

mum-careconcern.blogspot.co.uk

Sir Winston Churchill Remembered

 Yvonne Stewart Williams Butler
Just now · GoFundMe · 🏛

Sunday 24th January 2016 was the fifty-first
Anniversary of One of my all time Heroes and
greatest Prime Minister in History: Sir Winston
Churchill: Here I am having drinks while stand
proudly next to his grandson: Nicholas Soame

Married Gay Men With Mental Health
Yvonne Stewart Williams Butler has posted a new

Prison Number XR6890

mum-careconcern.blogspot.co.uk

More ▾   Next Blog»

CARE & CONCERN

SUNDAY, 24 JANUARY 2016

A Medal For My Beloved Son James

Today I enjoyed a few hours of unsupervised contact with my beloved son James, and was give

mum-careconcern.blogspot.co.uk

THURSDAY, 21 JANUARY 2016

My Change.Org Petition

https://www.facebook.com/yvonne.stewartwilliamsbutler/posts/101
53344902122596

Far too many Gay Males are attempting to complete suicide, lack of functional family community involvement, role models and mentors; and isolation due to loss of a loved one, age, stigma and discrimination.

In my Brixton, Coldharbour Ward, London, and nationally; we need confident Openly Gay males to be visible audible role models and mentors:

sons, brothers, grandsons, nephews, cousins, husbands, partners, carers, uncles, fathers, neighbours, friends, colleagues, overseers, elders, and associates

To our community in particular where often positive openly gay male role models are at a minimum and young males and females, as well as the older generation... Would benefit from Gay Males vital contribution

I am the lone lesbian mother of a heterosexual male teenager, who is an only child and believe my son and I would appreciate the constructive none threatening input openly gay males can provide.

Please create a Gay Male Commission to discover the causes of gay male suicides and ways of including gay in to the lives of the younger and older generation.

If we lose this campaign the loss would be infinite

If we win this campaign we create a greater society by fostering an inclusive community starting the family

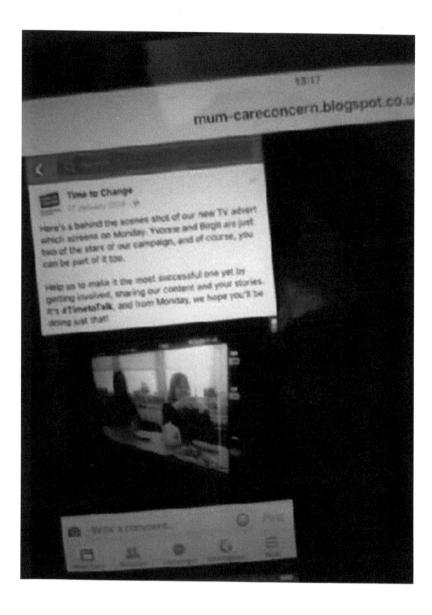

Prison Number XR6890

13:20

mum-careconcern.blogspot.co.uk

House Of Parliament Tour

O2-UK   07:11

...ories that you share here, we
thought that you'd like to look back on
this post from 1 year ago.

1 Year Ago

Prison Number XR6890

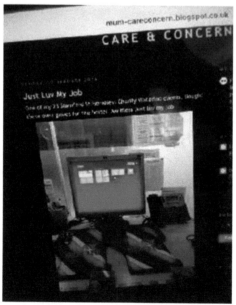

Prison Number XR6890

13:23

mum-careconcern.blogspot.co.uk

Rev Sharon Ferguson + Michael Cashman

Me wearing a Stonewall Trans T-shirt with Lord Michael Cashman on my left and Rev Sharon Ferguson on my right

✕   🏷️ 📍 ⋯

Me & Rev Sharon Ferguson and Lord Michael Cashman of Limehouse, today at the 4th

👍 Like   💬 Comment   ➡️ Share

Brighton England

I am grateful for my first visit to Brighton with my mother (see photo)and then my first visit to Brighton Pride with my beloved son James (see photo) and my first Duties in Brighton at the 2013 UNISON Lesbian, Gay, Bisexual & Transgender Union Brighton Conference, where I was pleased to hear Lord Michael Cashman speak. (Listen to my SoundCloud of his speech).

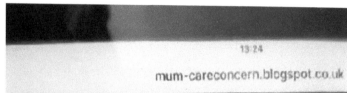

Prison Number XR6890

mum-careconcern.blogspot.co.uk

SATURDAY, 9 JANUARY 2016

My Brompton Bicycle

I am grateful for my Brompton Bicycle and cups of delicious English Breakfast Tea in my local area Ritzy Bar, Brixton Coldharbour Ward

Prison Number XR6890

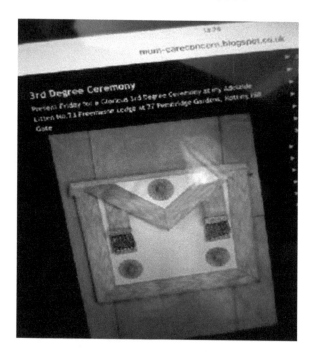

3rd Degree Ceremony

Present Friday for a Glorious 3rd Degree Ceremony at my Adelaide Litten No.71 Freemason Lodge at 77 Pembridge Gardens, Notting Hill Gate

mum-careconcern.blogspot.co.uk

My Apologies Sent

Sorry, unable to attend my Quaker Overseers Meeting on 14th January 2016, due to essential 73 Stamford St Homeless Charity Winter/no Work commitments

mum-careconcern.blogspot.co.uk

My OU-Open University Homework

Just now Had Breakfast Wearing Stonewall Uk Tshirt&Pyjamas in bed;
studying my OU-Open University DB123-15J On Apple

In Memory Of My Bisexual Stewart Namesake, King James I.

Amazing Grace   Romans 5:15, Psalm 66:16; John 9:25

Amazing grace! How sweet the sound
That saved a wretch like me!
I once was lost, but now am found;
Was blind, but now I see

'Twas Grace that taught my heart to fear,
And grace my fears relieved;
How precious did that grace appear
The hour I first believed.

Through many dangers, toils and snares,
I have already come.
'Tis grace hath brought me safe thus far
And grace will lead me home.

The Lord has promised good to me.
His Word my hope secures;
He will my Shield and Portion be,
As long as life endures.

Yea, when this flesh and heart shall fail,
And mortal life shall cease,
I shall possess, within the veil,
A life of joy and peace.

The earth shall soon dissolve like snow,
The sun forbear to shine;
But God, who called me here below,
Will be forever mine.

When we've been there ten thousand years,
Bright shining as the sun,
We've no less days to sing God's praise
Than when we'd first begun.

mum-careconcern.blogspot.co.uk

13:29

WEDNESDAY, 4 JANUARY 2016

My Lodge

I am happy to be with my Freemason lodge this Friday

Lodge Adelaide Litten No. 23
W. Bro. Cynthia H Ramsay
17th April 2015
Virtus et Lumen

Prison Number XR6890

Prison Number XR6890

Prison Number XR6890

Prison Number XR6890

13:35

erotomaniame.blogspot.co.uk

Rt Hon Nicholas Soames PC MP

Prison Number XR6890

Prison Number XR6890

Prison Number XR6890

erotomaniame.blogspot.co.uk

Posted by [...] at 10:45   No comments

Four in Ten

Four in Ten

South London and Maudsley
Lesbian, Gay, Bisexual, Trans Service User Group

It's hard to believe that Four in Ten is just one year old,
so much has happened: friendships have formed;
a film has been made; coming out stories have been
shared; our identity has emerged; and we're becoming
known throughout the local survivor and LGBT
communities.

Our plan for year two is to get bigger, better and more
fabulous [...] way.

Issue No 1

CONTENTS

4 in 10 a good thing that's happening
The Movie
Staff's Friendly Faces
Life, Experience & Hopes of a Transsexual Woman
Benefit Reassessments
My Vivian and me, Claude Cahun, LGBT Teens
Steve's Crossword, jokes
Queers Against the Cuts
Reporting LGBT Hate Crime

The Newsletter   Summer 2011

erotomaniame.blogspot.co.uk

Monday, 7 November 2011

Tower Bridge Magistrate Court

This morning, I attended Tower Bridge Magistrate Court. I was with three female friends and met my excellent solicitor Richard Grace, who was recommended to me by GALOP.

I was given a suspended sentence for two years, fined £85 and given a restraining order.

If Richard was not representing me, I would have been given a harsher sentence!

Posted by Erotomania & Me at 22:41   No comments:

Friday, 4 November 2011

Time To Change

Prison Number XR6890

erotomaniame.blogspot.co.uk

Schizophrenia Commission

Despite having a set back yesterday. It was seeing my general practitioner and finding out that my blood pressure is high.

However, today I participated in the launch of the Schizophrenia Commission, as I am one of the commissioners. It is a 100 years since the coining of the phrase Schizophrenia by the Swiss Psychiatrist Eugen Beuler. Please go to the following website to find out more about what the commission is about:

www.schizophreniacommission.org.uk

In addition, I read in the Daily Telegraph about the fact of Gay Civil partnerships will be allowed in Churches . from 5th December 2011. Hurrah!

http://www.stonewall.org.uk/media/current_releases/6556.asp

Posted by   at

Caroline Spelman MP

Prison Number XR6890

Altered Perception PODCAST

Today, I am enjoying a day in bed - alone. I am resting after a very busy week at work and at play.

I have decided to add my podcasts to various posts. Enjoy.

Posted by   at

2011 Birmingham Liberal Democrats' Party Conference.

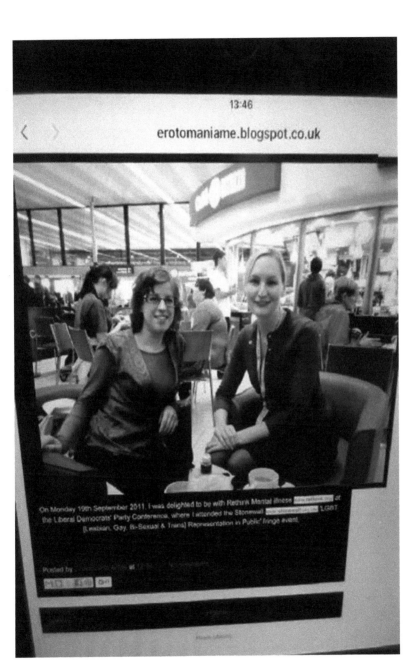

13:46

erotomaniame.blogspot.co.uk

On Monday 19th September 2011, I was delighted to be with Rethink Mental illness at the Liberal Democrats' Party Conference, where I attended the Stonewall LGBT (Lesbian, Gay, Bi-Sexual & Trans) Representation in Public' fringe event.

Posted by

lifeafterinprisonmentpsychiatrichosp blogspot.co.uk

LIFE AFTER INPRISONMENT PSYCHIATRIC HOSPITALS

THURSDAY, 4 FEBRUARY 2010

TWITTER

MY BLOG LIST

- Care & Concern
  Me & Justine Green
  6 months ago

- On the Cusp of Ma
  Time To Change
  8 years ago

- http://www.deveti
  mag

FOLLOWERS

Followers (1)

Follow

Heathen Massive UK, Gospel Dance Music for Lesbian, Gay, Bisexual and Transgendered Supporters. Feel free to donate to www.aidsmap.com

http://web.me.com/yvonnestewartwilli/Altered_Perception is my website where my podcasts can be found. Enjoy.

I have recently had my e-book Altered Perceptions published.

Here is the link

http://chipmunkapublishing.co.uk/shop/index.php?main_page=product_info&products_id=1547

BLOG ARCHIVE

▼ 2010 (2)
  ▼ February (1)
    Heathen Massive
    Dance Music fo
  ► January (1)
► 2009 (52)

Prison Number XR6890

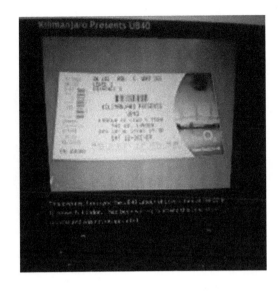

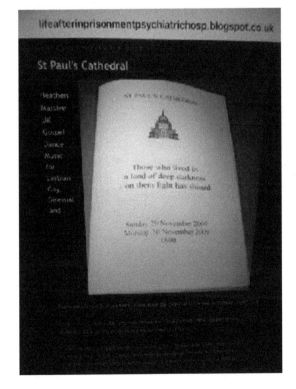

TUESDAY, 24 NOVEMBER 2009

Mind Mental Health Media Awards 2009

It has been one week and one day since my final discharge CPA from Eileen Skellen 3 Ward. Thursday I went to a Political discussion evening at my local Dulwich & West Norwood Conservative Party and on Saturday just past, I leaflet dropped and had lunch with them. This evening I accepted my RSVP place at the now MIND Mental Health Media Awards 2009, at BAFTA hosted by Shappi Khorsandi and was yet again delighted with the high quality of media coverage that mental health has received this year. Although in my mind they were all winners, I was pleased to see Alistair Campbell collect an award for BBC Two's Full length TV documentary Cracking Up' and an award going to BBC Two's TV news 'Mental Health in Parliament: Newsnight. The special award for More4 / True Vision Chosen: True Stories about child sexual abuse was well placed as was Eastenders' recognition.

Heathen Massive UK, Gospel Dance Music for Lesbian, Gay, Bisexual and Transgendered Supporters. Feel free to donate to

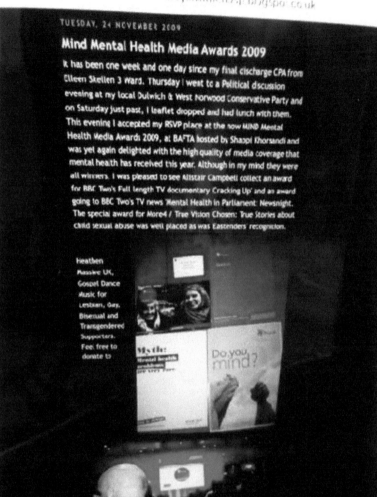

Prison Number XR6890

Prison Number XR6890

WEDNESDAY, 21 OCTOBER 2009

Krystal Online Magazine

Heathen Massive UK, Gospel Dance Music for Lesbian, Gay, Bisexual and Transgendered Supporter. Feel free to donate to www.aidsmap.com

Today I got my birthday card from my beloved son laminated. I am so thrilled that I rang and spoke to his social worker about it. After starting to read Practising The Power of NOW by Eckhart Tolle and listening to him on YouTube. Then I read my interview for Krystal http://www.krystalmag.co.uk/ It appeared in the Lifestyle section under the heading Black Mental Health: Never forget that they are there 20/10/2009. I followed this by tuning into [Speaker's Conference] Re: What is the best way to increase the representation of under-represented communities at Westminster? www.parliament.uk Today is also the wards Black History Month and World Mental Health Day Celebration. Lots of food and drinks and everyone seems to be having a great time.

13:54

lifeafterinprisonmentpsychiatrichosp.blogspot.co.uk

TUESDAY, 20 OCTOBER 2009

Hi Mum

Heathen
Massive UK,
Gospel Dance
Music for
Lesbian, Gay,
Bisexual and
Transgendered
Supporter. Feel
free to donate
to

www.aidsmap.com

Right now, I am wearing a big cheesy grin. It is because I have just been handed an envelope which contained inside a handmade birthday card from my beloved son. No surprises for guessing that the artwork were aircrafts, seventeen in total, some spitfires. The card had his writing: Hi Mum lots of love James xxx xxxx and Happy Birthday!!!

lifeafterinprisonmentpsychiatrichosp.blogspot.co.uk

My Beloved Son

Heathen Massive UK, Gospel Dance Music for Lesbian, Gay, Bisexual and Transgendered Supporter. Feel free to donate to www.aidsmap.com

Not one single day goes by, without me thinking about James, my beloved son. Today is no different. It has been too many months since I have spoken to him or seen him. It is one of the most heartbreaking things to happen to a parent like me on a locked psychiatric ward. Just what is happening for my dear son, goodness only knows.

At this time of day, and day of week, my son will be at school. I know that he has started to attend a new school because his social worker told me, when she visited me. I am pleased with the choice of school as when he was younger than one year of age he was christened in the same school. It is a Church of England school and now he will be wearing a school uniform and I have yet to hear what he thinks of this.

I love my son and loved him from before he was born. When he was only five days old following a caesarian section delivery both he and I transferred from St Thomas Hospital to the Bethlem Royal psychiatric Hospital's Mother and Baby Unit. This was just in case my mental health declined. It didn't. In the Mother and Baby unit my son and I bonded further and he took to his breastfeeding routine of hourly feeds day and night.

On further psychiatric hospital admissions, I wished that I could return to a place like the Mother and Baby unit, where I could go with my son. Just like respite care for HIV/AIDS mothers and their children. Unfortunately this type of facility was not available for mental health patients with children older than babies, so my child was placed in foster care.

LIFE AFTER INPRISONMENT & PSYCHIATRIC HOSPITALS

The Love That Dare Not Speak It's Name

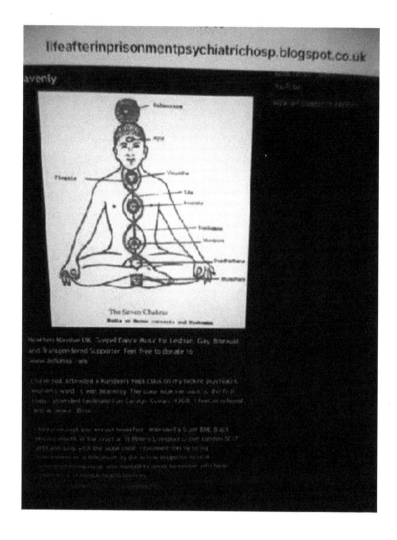

lifeafterinprisonmentpsychiatrichosp.blogspot.co.uk

lifeafterimprisonmentpsychiatrichosp.blogspot.co.uk

UESDAY, 13 OCTOBER 2009

Happy Birthday 2 Me

Age Is Like Underwear
48
It Creeps Up On You

Heathen Massive UK. Gospel Dance Music for Lesbian, Gay, Bisexual and Transgendered Supporter. Feel free to donate to www.aidsmap.com

I am having a great birthday today so far, mainly thanks to friends and my consultant psychiatrist. I went to a ward round yesterday and my consultant -a woman - said that I can have one hour of un-escorted leave each day [that was subject to clearing it with the police] I am also allowed to have my laptop and ipod touch returned to me via same police clearance. I am allowed to have my 30mls of trifluoperazine reduced by five mls to 25mls. All of the aforementioned started today except the medication which started the same day.

So today, I took the bus to my favourite Marks and Spencer to purchase cake for us patients and a few other bits and bobs. I have been making use of my mobile for the first time in months and included in it's use was a long overdue conversation with my dear old long suffering mum. When we got to the part of the conversation when she told me that she didn't know what had happened to me and then she received my prison letter - I laughed. [Sorry] then we both started laughing. It was such a pleasure to hear my mum's voice and the was so pleased to hear from me [busy as she is with her Jehovah's Witness ministry]

I then spoke to various friends, one of which [when I told her what had happened to me] told me that I seem to be a candidate for SLAA Sex and Love Addicts Anonymous - We both laughed for ages. It's so good to reconnect with the outside world.

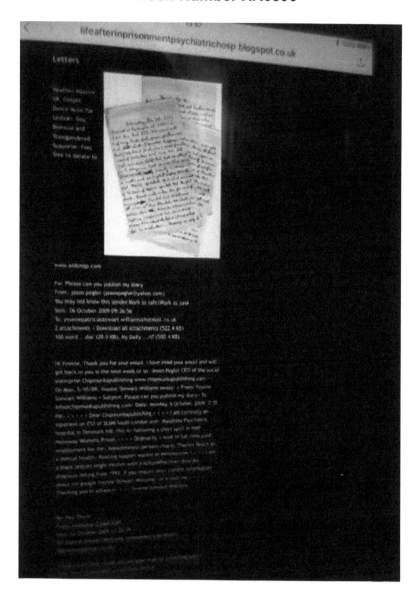

From: Yvonne Stewart-Williams
Date: Mon, 28 Sep 2009 14:29:13 +0100
To:
Subject: RE: Hey There

Hi dearest Linda,

Thank you for your e-mail.

I don't know how long I am going to be in hospital. I have been here since 20th August 2009. My line manager and manager are going to physically visit me on Friday 2nd October 2009 and my friend Birgit is going to visit me on Sunday 4th October 2009.

I have my suspicions that I will still be in here for my birthday on 13th October 2009. But hopefully I will be released soon after if not before. I am desperate to get to a meeting.

Much love

Yvonne

RE: What's happening?
From: Yvonne Stewart-Williams (yvonnepatriciastewart-williams@hotmail.co.uk)
Sent: 01 October 2009 16:36:21
To: peter.reveszd4hamesreach.org.uk

Hi Peter,

Thank you so much for your e-mail. I really do appreciate you taking time out to write.
I hope that you and yours are all okay.

Me, I am taking time out here in SLaM following a spell in HMP Holloway. What can I say?!! Except that you are probably lucky that you didn't have ME for a blood sister! However, I really miss you and your excellent sense of humour, straight forward logical approach and compassion.

I have just started reading the Eckhart Tolle book 'The Power of Now' and I am hoping that it is going to clarify things for me. It may seem like quite an odd thing for me to be saying following a prison experience bolted on to time in a psychiatric hospital but, I have never felt as much love in myself as I do now, despite my few down days!
Mind you, I have been visited by Ken and Emma this afternoon and told earlier that I will be getting a phone call from my son via social services.

You never guess what Peter? £33 ward has asked me to try to contact Frank Bruno to do a talk for mental health day - we a celebrating it here on 21st October. Imagine that? What can I do, when I couldn't even produce Frank for Thames Reach.

Anyway when you find a little time, please work your fine good healing magic and contact me again.

Give Park and big hug

From: Peter Revess<peter.revess@thamesreach.org.uk>
To: yvonnepatriciastewart-williams@hotmail.co.uk
Date: Fri, 2 Oct 2009 11:36:57 +0000
Subject: What's happening!

Hi Yvonne,
Just a quick one to say how's it hanging!
Long time no hear.
I hope you are ok!
Best wishes,
Peter.

Peter Revess
Practical Support Worker

Thames Reach
Westminster Mental Health Floating Support Scheme
22-33 Scrutton Ground
London SW1P 2HZ

T 020 7064 6832

M 07725 823 905
W www.thamesreach.org.uk

Ü Before printing, think about the environment

Southwark Mind LGBT project
From: Denise McKenna (denise_mckenna1@btopenworld.com)
Sent: 28 September 2009 17:21:51
To: flavia.silva@pacehealth.org.uk
Cc: Yvonne (YvonnePatriciaStewart-williams@hotmail.co.uk)

Hi Flavia,

We spoke earlier today about an LGBT project/group which users in Southwark Mind are wishing to set up. The idea of the project emerged from a small user/survivor group called the Rainbow Resource which started in a day centre in Southwark a few years ago

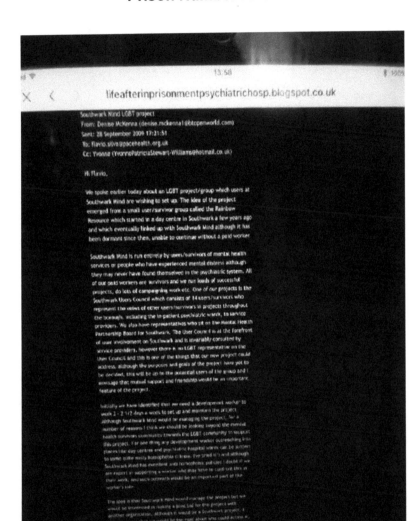

Southwark Mind LGBT project

From: Denise McKenna (denise.mckenna1@btopenworld.com)

Sent: 28 September 2009 17:21:51

To: flavio.silva@spacehealth.org.uk

Cc: Yvonne (YvonnePatriciaStewart-Williams@hotmail.co.uk)

Hi Flavio,

We spoke earlier today about an LGBT project/group which users at Southwark Mind are wishing to set up. The idea of the project emerged from a small user/survivor group called the Rainbow Resource which started in a day centre in Southwark a few years ago and which eventually linked up with Southwark Mind although it has been dormant since then, unable to continue without a paid worker.

Southwark Mind is run entirely by users/survivors of mental health services or people who have experienced mental distress although they may never have found themselves in the psychiatric system. All of our paid workers are survivors and we run loads of successful projects, do lots of campaigning work etc. One of our projects is the Southwark Users Council which consists of 14 users/survivors who represent the voice of other users/survivors in projects throughout the borough, including the in-patient psychiatric wards, to service providers. We also have representatives who sit on the Mental Health Partnership Board for Southwark. The User Council is at the forefront of user involvement on Southwark and is invariably consulted by service providers, however there is no LGBT representative on the User Council and this is one of the things that our new project could address, although the purpose and goals of the project have yet to be decided, this will be up to the potential users of the group and I envisage that mutual support and friendship would be an important feature of the project.

Initially we have identified that we need a development worker to work 1 - 2 1/2 days a week to set up and monitor the project. Although Southwark Mind would be managing the project, for a number of reasons I think we should be looking beyond the mental health survivors community towards the LGBT community to support this project. For one thing any development worker outreaching into places like day centres and psychiatric hospital wards can be subject to some quite nasty homophobia I know. I've tried it's evil although Southwark Mind has excellent anti-homophobic policies I doubt if we are expert in supporting a worker who may have to carry out this in their work, and such outreach would be an important part of the worker's role.

The idea is that Southwark Mind would manage the project but we would be interested in making a joint bid for the project with another organisation, although it would be a Southwark project. I don't envisage that we would be too rigid about who could access it, for example, Southwark Mind has strong links with Lambeth Mind and Lambeth users who might also want to use the project.

[illegible faded lines]

[illegible faded lines]

We hope to have a focus group, which would be paid for my Southwark Mind (we don't envisage it would cost much) some time in December to establish the need for the project for the purposes of any bid and wonder if you might be able to provide us with any help in setting this up, if only in the form of advice and planning!

We would be very grateful to hear of any support you could give us in setting up this project and any thoughts you might have about it.

Thanks and best wishes
Denise McKenna
Southwark Mind

POSTED BY IRC WIG AT 14:20 NO COMMENTS:

SATURDAY, 3 OCTOBER 2009

Johnathan Livingstone Seagull

Heathen Massive UK, Gospel Dance Music for Lesbian, Gay, Bisexual and Transgendered Supporter. Feel free to donate to www.aidsmap.com

I paused in between reading 'The Power of Now' to watch the film 'Johnathan Livingston Seagull' which I had previously downloaded from Itunes, on my ipod classic. I remained in the now and was truly satisfied.

Yesterday produced a catalyst for change which has continued today. Earlier, this fine day, I visited the forces store on Walworth road accompanied by a nurse from the ward and purchased a few items. It was good to be out with everyone else.

Today I again got in touch with deep seated feelings of LOVE and just now the LOVE feelings was experienced by me again. I believe that I am experiencing an advanced enhanced me and LOVE is a key point to my being. It sounds a bit wobble and particularly when I consider that I am on a locked psychiatric ward, and not too long ago I was locked up in HMP Holloway. But it's true.

To be quite frank, it was hard for me to watch Johnathon Livingston Seagull, as I felt as if I was with Johnathon on his journey a bit like one of the Outcasts. I suppose what I am saying is that learning to not develop a fear of the future is going to be very important process for me. I must return to society, but the longer this is delayed the harder it seems. What I am trying to convey in my writing is that the possibility of my becoming institutionalised is an even present concern in my mind. However, one day at a time, I continue reading The power of now and remembering that I am human and not different.

And fly lucky, with a seagull. Johnathon Livingston seagull & Jospet

Prison Number XR6890

lifeafterinprisonmentpsychiatrichosp.blogspot.co.uk

PSYCHIATRIC HOSPITALS

FRIDAY, 2 OCTOBER 2009

I Feel Fine

Heathen Massive UK, Gospel Dance Music for Lesbian, Gay, Bisexual and Transgendered Supporter. Feel free to donate to www.aidsmap.com

Today has produced seeds of truths to yeald beyond my wildest dreams! First of all my psychiatrist told me that I will be having an interview on Tuesday at 4pm for assessment for psychotherapy. Then my son's Social Worker rang me on the ward's patient phone and after telling me all about my son, and me satisfying myself that all is as well with him as could be under the current set of circumstances, she has made an appointment to visit me on Wednesday at 2pm. Then I went into group therapy today and was given the Eckhart Tolle book The Power of NOW? and I have started reading it because I was told, I looked as if I lacked sleep and seemed depressed (surprise, surprise). Then my managers visited me today and placed a new down on a new day. Another good thing is I have been granted two half hour sessions of accompanied leave each day (subject to staff availability) Bad news, still unable to record my podcasts.

POSTED BY THE MTG AT 19:24 NO COMMENTS:

THURSDAY, 1 OCTOBER 2009

'That's What Friends Are For'

Heathen Massive UK, Gospel Dance Music For Lesbian, Gay, Bisexual and Transgendered Supporter. Feel free to donate to www.aidsmap.com

RE: Hey There
From: Yvonne Stewart-Williams (yvonnepohrinaustewart-williams@hotmail.co.uk)
Sent: 28 September 2009 04:29:13
To: lindeemail2@aack.com

Hi dearest kinds,

Thank you for your e-mail.

I don't know how long I am going to be on hospital. I have been here since 20th August 2009. My care managers and manager are going for physio why visit me on Friday 2nd October 2009 and my friend Birgit is going to visit me on Tuesday 4th October 2009

I have my outpatients that I will still be in here for my birthday on 18th October 2009. But hopefully I will be released soon when if not before. I am looking out to get to a meeting

TWITTER

MY BLOG LIST

Care & Concern
Me & Justice Grooving MP
6 months ago

On the Cusp of Madness
Time To Change
3 years ago

http://www.devotion.co.uk/.mag

FOLLOWERS

Followers (1)

BLOG ARCHIVE

▼ 2010 (2)
  ▼ February (1)
    Heathen Massive UK, Gospel Dance Music for Lesbia...
  ► January (1)
► 2009 (52)

ABOUT ME

I am a London England born Black Lesbian Single mother of my beloved kindergt of money bereaved son, Jessey and I am one of justice on Heritage. I have lived experiences of Psychiatric Hospitalisation due to a Schizoaffective disorder Mental Health diagnosis. I have Spent time in and the care Prison Staff Suddenin. Women's Prison due to breakdown. I am an avoid Liberal and supporter of London, Gay, Bisexual & Transgendered. View my work under Lesbian representation on YouTube.

View my complete profile

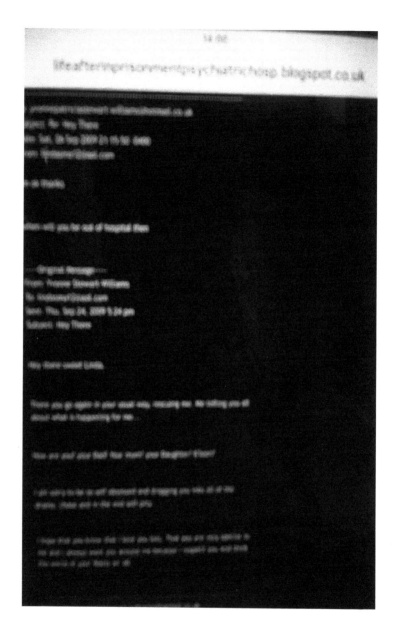

From: yvonnepatriciastewart-williams@hotmail.co.uk
To: lindasma12@aol.com
Subject: FW: Greetings!
Date: Tue, 22 Sep 2009 19:34:23 +0100

Dearest Linda,

I sincerely hope that I have not frightened you away, with the baby
love history.

To be honest, I did try throughout this five years of being in love with
Carolyn to find a suitable alternative love interest. For instance, I
subscribed to one year of 'Gaydar Girls', and dined out at Fortnum &
Mason's for afternoon tea, with one woman that I had met from that
online dating service.

It can appear as if I was dragging my feet over finding a suitable
girlfriend, by staying celibate for six years and seem as if I was doing
nothing. But, I was and am lovelorn and broken inside and couldn't,
can't keep verbalizing it. In a way things had to come to a head for
me to find some peace within.

I don't know what my future holds as far as 'Love' is concerned. I just
know that I love Carolyn and if she was available, I would be on top
of the world. I guess that I am similar to everyone else and would like
a monogamous, caring, productive, loving, sexually stimulating,
honest, respectful, romantic relationship with a woman built on
trust.

I want to cuddle up with that someone special and be hugged by that
someone special. I have a reputation for giving the best hugs in NA.
Yet I have never even shook hands with Carolyn let alone given her
one of my hugs! It's sad really Linda, not that I cry myself to sleep or
anything like that, but it is along those lines.

I so want to walk in your footsteps Linda but it's so hard. I know that I
won't try hard enough with the wrong woman. I won't accept abuse. I
have to love her.

From: yvonnepatriciastewart-williams@hotmail.co.uk

Okay Linda, here we go,

To understand how I ended up in prison, I need to take you back just over five years.

I had been in this same psychiatric hospital. Feeling like Uma Thurman in the Tarrantino movie 'Kill Bill' after social services had removed my only beloved biological son James from my full time care. I was assigned Ros Ramsey, a female Consultant Psychiatrist for the first time and after initially not caring one way or another because I was too distraught. I noticed her professionalism and idiosyncratic approach. Developed an unrequited crush and became smitten. By the time I came off my section I was writing to her in prose and poetry. Although I could not remember what colour her eyes were and at this stage in time, I cannot remember what she looks like b ut I still remember her professionalism.

Then, when I got my son back a few months later, and I took him back to his Rudolf Steiner School and met some new parents. One of which was Carolyn Cowan [HUGO] She introduced herself to me. I didn't think anything of it especially as I could not remember her christian name! and kept calling her Caroline. Carolyn offered to give my son and myself lifts to school on the school runs, invited me to her home for meals with her husband, family and friends, and events. I purchased her DVD's and goods from her online stores and her shop and my son played with her two children Louis HUGO and Isadora HUGO and I took her son Louis out on excursions with my son James.

After dining with Carolyn, I emailed her and told her that I adored her. Carolyn explained that she felt my actions were harassment. That news was relayed through my son's school to my psychiatrist & Mental Health Social Worker and I was spoken to about it. Carolyn distanced herself and then things resumed as per usual but I was then hospitalised again in this psychiatric hospital.

This time I did not get my son back and I was not allowed to return to his school. But I continued to pay my son's school fees.

When I went into recovery I placed Carolyn on my step four but by this time it came to it I knew I did not want to make amends and contacted her again. I started buying things again from her shop and buying things and sending them to her ie flowers, e-mails, texts, cards . Then one day I rang to make a work related suggestion and she answered the phone and told me for the second time that she felt my actions were harassment.

I went to her shop. she called the police. I was arrested and a Harassment notice was served. I returned to her shop two days later having wrote a Carolyn I would break this notice and not again and . . . Spent the night in a police cell. Went to court the next . . . and stood out this judge that I would stay away from Carolyn

lifeafterinprisonmentpsychiatrichosp.blogspot.co.uk

To: yvonnepatriciastewart-williams@hotmail.co.uk
Subject: Re: Greetings!
Date: Thu, 17 Sep 2009 23:23:20 -0400
From: lindasma12@aol.com

hi there a
so why dont you fill me in in the email let me know what has
happened to you write like a baby life story
how did you end up in a jail

lots of love to you

-----Original Message-----
From: Yvonne Stewart-Williams
To: lindasma12@aol.com
Sent: Thu, Sep 17, 2009 6:22 pm
Subject: RE: Greetings!

Dearest Linda,

Lovely to hear from you. Fabulous news that you are abroad.
Hopefully with plenty of sun.

I truly am sorry that I worried you. I feel better now that I have made
contact with you. I visualize you and I feel reassured that one day at
a time, things will work out.

Thank you for being you

Much love

Yvonne

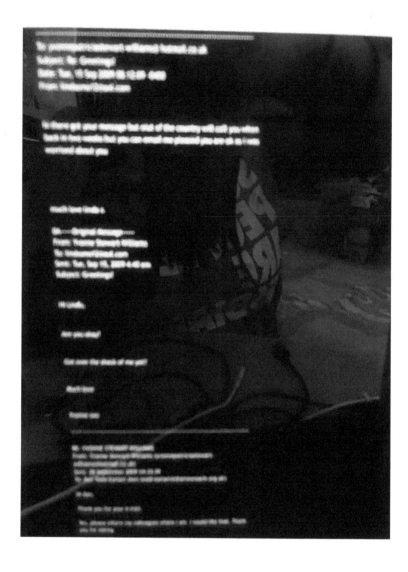

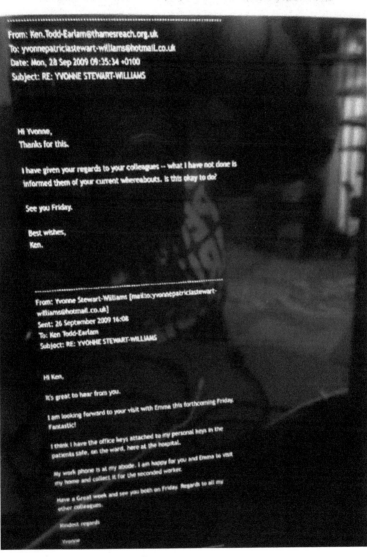

From: Ken.Todd-Earlam@thamesreach.org.uk
To: yvonnepatriciastewart-williams@hotmail.co.uk
Date: Mon, 28 Sep 2009 09:35:34 +0100
Subject: RE: YVONNE STEWART-WILLIAMS

Hi Yvonne,
Thanks for this.

I have given your regards to your colleagues -- what I have not done is
informed them of your current whereabouts. Is this okay to do?

See you Friday.

Best wishes,
Ken.

From: Yvonne Stewart-Williams [mailto:yvonnepatriciastewart-
williams@hotmail.co.uk]
Sent: 26 September 2009 16:08
To: Ken Todd-Earlam
Subject: RE: YVONNE STEWART-WILLIAMS

Hi Ken,

It's great to hear from you.

I am looking forward to your visit with Emma this forthcoming Friday.
Fantastic!

I think I have the office keys attached to my personal keys in the
patients safe, on the ward, here at the hospital.

My work phone is at my abode. I am happy for you and Emma to visit
my home and collect it for the seconded worker.

Have a Great week and see you both on Friday. Regards to all my
other colleagues.

Kindest regards

Yvonne

From: Ken.Todd-Earlam@thamesreach.org.uk
To: yvonnepatriciastewart-williams@hotmail.co.uk
CC: Mike.Archeti-Green@thamesreach.org.uk
Date: Fri, 25 Sep 2009 18:01:41 +0100
Subject: RE: YVONNE STEWART-WILLIAMS

Hello Yvonne,

Hope this finds you well.

I am sorry I missed your two p[hone calls. Good to hear that you are feeling in a good space.

I plan to visit you on Friday October 2nd. between 2pm & 8pm. If possible, I need to get your work phone and office keys as we currently have a short-term secondment filling your post.

I plan to bring Emma along with me.

I hope this is okay with you.

Please let me know if you will not be available for as visit during that time.

Best wishes,

Ken.

From: Yvonne Stewart-Williams [mailto:yvonnepatriciastewart-williams@hotmail.co.uk]
Sent: 09 September 2009 17:59
To: Ken Todd-Earlam
Subject: RE: YVONNE STEWART-WILLIAMS

Ken,

Apologies. Here are my visiting hours are:

Mornings - 10:00 - 11.30

Afternoons - 14:00 - 17:00

Evenings - 18:30 - 20:00

Prison Number XR6890

From: Ken.Todd-Earlam@thamesreach.org.uk
To: yvonnepatriciastewart-williams@hotmail.co.uk
Date: Mon, 7 Sep 2009 15:03:16 +0100
Subject: RE: YVONNE STEWART-WILLIAMS

Thanks Yvonne,

I will check when I am able to visit, and let you know.

Best wishes,

Ken.

> From: Yvonne Stewart-Williams [mailto:yvonnepatriciastewart-
> williams@hotmail.co.uk]
> Sent: 03 September 2009 14:57
> To: Ken Todd-Earlam
> Subject: RE: YVONNE STEWART-WILLIAMS

> Hi Ken,

> The visiting hours are 11:00 to 20:00

> Kindest regards,

> Yvonne

>> From: Ken.Todd-Earlam@thamesreach.org.uk
>> To: yvonnepatriciastewart-williams@hotmail.co.uk
>> Date: Mon, 7 Sep 2009 12:20:50 +0100
>> Subject: RE: YVONNE STEWART-WILLIAMS

>> Hi Yvonne,

>> Good to hear from you and to know that you are moving / settling
>> well.

>> Please can that visiting hours there?

>> Cheers,
>> Ken.

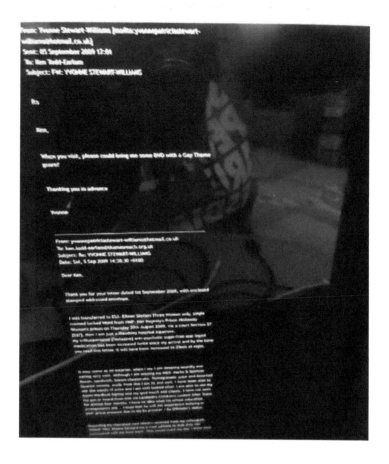

From: Yvonne Stewart-Williams [mailto:yvonnepatriciastewart-williams@hotmail.co.uk]
Sent: 05 September 2009 17:04
To: Ken Todd-Earlam
Subject: FW: YVONNE STEWART-WILLIAMS

Its

Ken,

When you visit, please could bring me some DVD with a Gay Theme genre?

Thanking you in advance

Yvonne

From: yvonnepatriciastewart-williams@hotmail.co.uk
To: ken.todd-earlam@thamesreach.org.uk
Subject: Re: YVONNE STEWART-WILLIAMS
Date: Sat, 5 Sep 2009 14:38:30 +0100

Dear Ken,

Thank you for your letter dated 1st September 2009, with enclosed stamped addressed envelope.

I was transferred to ESJ- Eileen Skellen Three women only, single roomed locked Ward from HMP, per Majesty's Prison Holloway Women's prison on Thursday 20th August 2009, via a court Section 37 [S37]. How I am just a Maudsley hospital inpatient.
My tri-fluoroperazine [Stelazine] anti-psychotic sugar-free oral liquid medication has been increased twice since my arrival, and by the time you read this letter, it will have been increased to 20mls at night.

Dear Ken,

Thank you for your letter dated 1st September 2009, with enclosed stamped addressed envelope.

I was transferred to ES3- Eileen Skellen Three Women only, single roomed locked Ward from HMP- Her Majesty's Prison Holloway Women's prison on Thursday 20th August 2009, via a court Section 37 [S37]. Now I am just a Maudsley hospital inpatient.
My trifluoperazine [Stelazine] anti-psychotic sugar-free oral liquid medication has been increased twice since my arrival and by the time you read this letter, it will have been increased to 25mls at night.

It may come as no surprise, when I say I am sleeping soundly and eating very well. Although I am missing my M&S- Marks & Spencer Bacon, sandwich, lemon cheesecake, Pomegranate juice and Assorted licorice sweets. Aside from this I am fit and well. I have been able to use the ward's IT suite and I am well looked after. I am able to use my Apple MacBook laptop and my ipod touch and classic. I have not seen my son or heard from him via Lambeth's Children's Looked After Team for almost four months. I have no idea what his school education arrangements are... I trust that he will not experience bullying or peer group pressure due to my Ex prisoner / Ex Offender's status.

Regarding my cherished card which I received from my colleagues, THANK YOU. Please forward my e-mail address so that they can correspond with me from work. That would make my day. I know they are busy, so what ever they can write would be respected.

I look forward to your visit. Choose a time which can accommodate your outlook calendar.

Kindest regards

Scotty ,

Prison Number XR6890

FW: Southwark Mind LGBT project
From: Yvonne Stewart-Williams (yvonnepatriciastewart-
williams@hotmail.co.uk)
Sent: 28 September 2009 14:40:38
To: denise.mckenna1@btopenworld.com

Dear Denise,

Hope all is well with you.

Thank you for cc'ing me into this e-mail. I am very interested in your
proposal and will do everything that I can to help.

It was great to see you again. As I said when I saw you, stay in touch.

Much love

Yvonne

Date: Sun, 27 Sep 2009 16:09:40 +0000
From: denise.mckenna1@btopenworld.com
Subject: Southwark Mind LGBT project
To: dax.ashworth@southwark.gov.uk
CC: YvonnePatriciaStewart-Williams@hotmail.co.uk

Hi Dax,

lifeafterimprisonmentpsychiatrichosp.blogspot.co.uk

Although Southwark Mind would manage the project, for all sorts of reasons I think we should be looking beyond the mental health survivors community towards the LGBT community to support this project. For one thing any development worker outreaching into places like day centres and hospitals can be subject to some nasty homophobia (I know, I've tried it) and outreach work would be a large part of the developemnt worker's role. As such it might be helpful if the worker was supported by more than one organisation. (Southwark Mind are not experts in dealing with homophobia and LGBT community input would be helpful). People with mental health problems can feel excluded from mainstream communities and I'm afraid that can even include the LGBT community. Who knows, the activities of the group could even include mental health awareness within the LGBT community.

Phew! So that's story. The questions are these: Do you know any organisation that might be interested in puting in a joint bid with Southwark Mind for this project? We plan to set up a Focus Group to demonstrate the need for such a project for the purposes of puting in a bid. Hopefully the focus group will be in Decemeber - S Mind would fund the focus group. Do you know of anyone who might want to be involved in helping us with this? Can you think of anyone in the LGBT community who might be interested in helping out with setting up this project? They needn't be professionals in any way, just someone with time on their hands who might want to help out. All of us LGBT survivors can be a bit fragile at times and this has slowed us down in getting this project off the ground and S Mind workers are currently tied up with funding and other issues relating to existing projects but recognise that an LGBT project is desperately needed. We could use all the help we can get.

Best wishes
Denise McKenzie
Southwark Mind

From: hildegund39@hotmail.com
To: yvonnepatriciastewart-williams@hotmail.co.uk
Subject: RE: Peacejavascript:;e One Day
Date: Tue, 29 Sep 2009 14:09:00 +0000

Hi Yvonne,

It was so lovely to talk to you over the phone on Sunday.

I am looking forward to visiting you this coming Sunday - I will be there at 2pm - can't wait to see you.

Sorry for the rushed e-mail - my internet at home is still not working and I am leaving work now...
Just a quick Hello and see you very soon.

Lots of love and strength

Birgit XX
Sept For Peace Day on 21 September...
I will tell everyone about peace one day and celebrate at the royal albert hall on 21 september what will you do! Visit
www.peaceoneday.org

From: yvonnepatriciastewart-williams@hotmail.co.uk
To: hildegund39@hotmail.com
Subject: RE: Peacejavascript:;e One Day
Date: Sat, 26 Sep 2009 16:12:39 +0100

Hi Birgit,

Thank you for your e-mail.

Speak soon, big hellos love and strength, my line manager are going to give to give me on Friday 2nd October 2009. Between 9am-5pm.

I look forward to hearing from you via telephone on Sunday

Lots of love

xxxxxx

Prison Number XR6890

Hi Yvonne

Thanks so much for your response. I am really thrilled by what you have written and so pleased that my coaching style has worked for you.

I will pass your contact details on to Rader.

I will fill you in on the dissertation another time - slightly weighed under with work right now! Remind me if I forget.

I am going to send you good thoughts and hope you will be out well before your birthday. I don't practise Buddhism, but I find their philosophy and approach to life very generative. Meditation is very helpful too. Calming and gives me a sense of space.

Let me know what happens won't you.

Thank you so much again

nicole

-----Original Message-----
From: Yvonne Stewart-Williams [mailto:yvonnepatriciastewart-williams@hotmail.co.uk]
Sent: 01 October 2009 11:35 AM
To: Veeah Nicole
Subject: RE: One Day At A Time

Dear Nicole,

Thank you for your e-mail.

It is lovely to hear from you. I think that it is fantastic to hear you using buddhist philosophy as a way forward for positive healing. I am also pleased that you are into trees and can appreciate their soothing qualities.

As for mental health, I am tiring of the institutionalisation and could personally do with practicing a bit of buddhism myself as, it is my birthday on the 13th of this month and I would like to have been released before then. My managers from my Thames Reach employers are physically visiting me tomorrow afternoon and I am hoping to see my psychiatrist today.

In addition thank you for your short concise explanation of your dissertation. After a very brief contemplation, I have decided to accept your invitation of a more generous helping. To be honest, to me the topic of your dissertation is so YOU: Communication, Clarification and Appropriate Effective Explanation and Execution. In corporate settings. To be quite frank it takes me back to your effective Radar coaching.

Which was, Outstanding because:

You were - Appropriate. Punctual. Prepared. Flexible. Professional. Compassionate. Intelligent. Resourceful. Honest.

You were a hard task master, but I was always sure that I was the centre of your focus. You allowed me to locate and concentrate my mind on the task in hand, and that was to achieve the maximum within that time we spent together, with far reaching effective consequences.

You had the superior quality of being able to unearth skills in me that I had hidden under a bushel and forgotten. You sowed new seeds in my mind and showed me how to nurture and grow them. You inspired confidence and produced the correct balance between carrot and stick. You were NO nanny. You inspired results, you conveyed this and got them.

You have a great sense of humour and your appearance is easy on the eye.

Maybe this phenomenon used is a synopsis of your attributes as a Radar coach, I am happy to write them, but I don't want people to steal that you are looking for.

Write again when you can find some time.

Warmest regards,

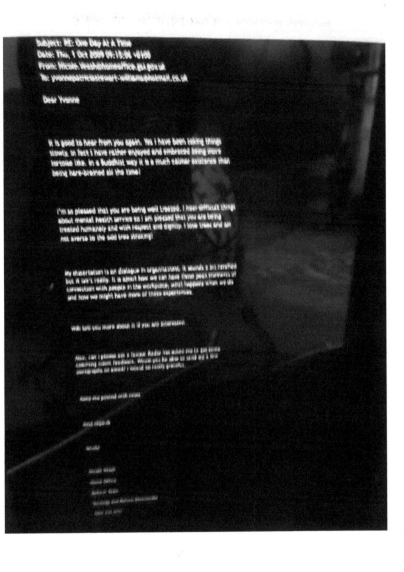

Subject: RE: One Day At A Time
Date: Thu, 1 Oct 2009 09:15:06 +0100
From: Nicole.Weah@homeoffice.gsi.gov.uk
To: yvonnepatriciastewart-williams@hotmail.co.uk

Dear Yvonne

It is good to hear from you again. Yes I have been taking things slowly, in fact I have rather enjoyed and embraced being more tortoise like. In a Buddhist way it is a much calmer existence than being hare-brained all the time!

I'm so pleased that you are being well treated. I hear difficult things about mental health service so I am pleased that you are being treated humanely and with respect and dignity. I love trees and am not averse to the odd tree stroking!

My dissertation is on dialogue in organisations. It sounds a bit rarefied but it isn't really. It is about how we can have those peak moments of connection with people in the workplace, what happens when we do and how we might have more of those experiences.

Will tell you more about it if you are interested.

Also, can I please see a Tascan Radar has asked me to get some calming colour feedback. Would you be able to send me a few paragraphs on email? I would be really grateful.

Keep me posted with news

And stay ok

Nicole

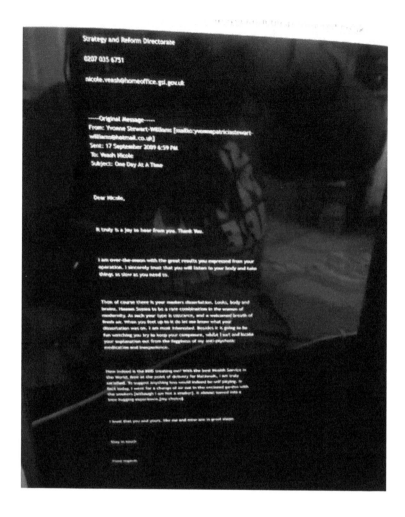

Strategy and Reform Directorate

0207 035 6751

nicole.veash@homeoffice.gsi.gov.uk

-----Original Message-----
From: Yvonne Stewart-Williams [mailto:yvonnepatriciastewart-williams@hotmail.co.uk]
Sent: 17 September 2009 4:59 PM
To: Veash Nicole
Subject: One Day At A Time

Dear Nicole,

It truly is a joy to hear from you. Thank You.

I am over-the-moon with the great results you expressed from your operation. I sincerely trust that you will listen to your body and take things as slow as you need to.

Then of course there is your masters dissertation. Looks, body and brains. Hassan Seems to be a rare combination in the women of modernity. As such your type is unscarce, and a welcomed breath of fresh air. When you feel up to it do let me know what your dissertation was on. I am most interested. Besides it is going to be fun watching you try to keep your composure, whilst I sort and locate your explanation text from the fogginess of my anti-psychotic medication and inexperience.

How indeed is the NHS treating me? With the best Health Service in the world, here at the point of delivery for Mailsmith, I am truly satisfied. To suggest anything less would indeed be self pitying. In fact today, I went for a change of air out in the enclosed garden with the smokers [although I am not a smoker]. It almost turned into a tree hugging experience. [my choice]

I trust that you and yours, like me and mine are in great shape.

Stay in touch

Fond regards

lifeafterinprisonmentpsychiatrichosp.blogspot.co.uk

TUESDAY, 29 SEPTEMBER 2009

Where did Chief go?

Heathen Massive UK, Gospel Dance Music for Lesbian, Gay, Bisexual and Transgendered Supporter. Feel free to donate to www.aidsmap.com

Let's get this straight. This is NOT a picnic. It is an acute NHS Psychiatric Ward in the capital of one the most major citys in the World.

I have been here on this ward for almost six weeks, following almost eight weeks in a Prison. Different. This very morning a patient did the [full monty]stripped naked and started walking around the ward before breakfast!

I see myself as a mere actor on this ward - In Shakespeare's words strutting on stage - as such I am playing Jack Nickleson's role in One Flew Over the Cuckoo's Nest and to be quite frank, at this moment in time I am seriously looking for the Chief with his pillow!

The constant broken sleep, shouting, banging, screaming, slamming, crying, mayhem, chaos, drama, stresses and petty squabbles distresses me. Almost beyond my more than ample capacity. I am teetering on the brink of insanity without any hope of return. After all this noise and confusion, Just the mere tip toe of a professional footstep would be likely to push me over the edge! Even a month of idle days filled with British Quaker meetings could not satisfy the silence, peace and serenity which I now crave!

lifeafterinprisonmentpsychiatrichosp.blogspot.co.uk

LIVE · EVIL

Heathen Massive UK, Gospel Dance Music for
Lesbian, Gay, Bisexual and Transgendered
Supporter. Feel free to donate to
www.aidsmap.com

SEX
HOLLYWOOD
POLITICS
SCIENCE
THE NEXT BIG THING
GOOD STUFF
WEB WORK

14:06

lifeafterinprisonmentpsychiatrichosp.blogspot.co.uk

MONDAY, 28 SEPTEMBER 2009

'Animal Farm'

Heathen Massive UK, Gospel Dance Music for
Lesbian, Gay, Bisexual and Transgendered
Supporter. Feel free to donate to
www.aidsmap.com

George Orwell may well have had a point with
'Animal Farm', as I found out this weekend on
this locked women's psychiatric ward.
Mayhem, Chaos and Confusion was the order of
the day, and that was just the patients! My nerves!?! I can hardly take
anymore.

I now believe that I am in a Mental Health Zoo ward, and I have the
split personality of a stressed out doberman pincher bitch and a
boxer bitch. Which aside from horses are my favourite animals.
After being abruptly woken up very early this morning with a patient
describing herself as a nurse, switching on my bedroom lights and
talking to me. This is on the back of my having gone to bed after
midnight. On closer examination of this patient (who had arrived on
the ward sometime during the night) I found that she was blowing me
kisses. Later in the morning another patient (did a moonie) took her
knickers down and bared her bare bottom directly in front of my
face! After I got over the shock, I wrote the following:

Caro

Although I know
it is always darkest before the dawn
I would be
the last to leave you...
As when I look into
your penetratively beautiful blue eyes
- a treat too rare -
your gaze
massages my metaphorical balls
and
has me endlessly climaxing
the unending,
never ending
Orgasm
Caro
Implicitly
I Love You

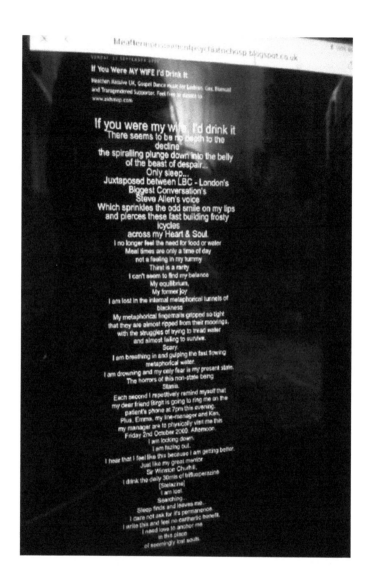

Prison Number XR6890

Only sleep...
Juxtaposed between LBC - London's
Biggest Conversation's
Steve Allen's voice
Which sprinkles the odd smile on my lips
and pierces these fast building frosty
icycles
across my Heart & Soul.
I no longer feel the need for food or water
Meal times are only a time of day
not a feeling in my tummy
Thirst is a rarity
I can't seem to find my balance
My equilibrium.
My former joy
I am lost in the internal metaphorical tunnels of
blackness
My metaphorical fingernails gripped so tight
that they are almost ripped from their moorings,
with the struggles of trying to tread water
and almost failing to survive.
Scary.
I am breathing in and gulping the fast flowing
metaphorical water.
I am drowning and my only fear is my present state.
The horrors of this non-state being
Stasis.
Each second I repetitively remind myself that
my dear friend Birgit is going to ring me on the
patient's phone at 7pm this evening.
Plus, Emma, my line-manager and Ken,
my manager are to physically visit me this
Friday 2nd October 2009. Afternoon.
I am locking down.
I am fazing out.
I hear that I feel like this because I am getting better.
Just like my great mentor
Sir Winston Churhill.
I drink the daily 30mls of trifluoperazine
[Stelazine]
I am lost.
Searching...
Sleep finds and leaves me...
I dare not ask for it's permanence.
I write this and feel no carthartic benefit.
I need love to anchor me
in this place
of seemingly lost souls.
I need LOVE.
I must find it within.

LIFE AFTER INPRISONMENT & PSYCHIATRIC HOSPITALS

SATURDAY, 24 SEPTEMBER 2009

One In The Cuckoos' Nest

Heathen Massive UK, Gospel Dance Music for Lesbian, Gay, Bisexual and Transgendered Supporter. Feel free to donate to www.odbmap.com

30mls of Trifluoperazine [Stelazine], at 10.00hrs every evening. Now, I just want to sleep my life away.

It's one of these days. They are rare for me, but I can feel it coming all the way from yesterday. It's hard. I am not keeping it in the day, one day at a time. It is not a just for today approach. It's self-pitying and relentlessly challenging. Help!

The school of hard knocks are teaching hard headed me another lesson in life. The locked ward has been drowning in a cacophony of sounds which has clashed terribly with my iPod classic, working it's way through more than eight thousand tracks. All low spirit, all big of depression and all darkest abyss at this moment in time, in my life.

I am not lonely, far from it. I have access to a number of people all day one time, day and night. But I don't want them. I don't want the reason. I am distressed, but yet seek more solitude. I have not physically entered a twelve step meeting since the end of June. I am aware that I have been surviving on a sprinkling of recovery crumbs in my brain box and saying the Serenity Prayer. I need help!

I am in desperate need of the still quiet voice of reason. A Quaker meeting for Worship. No mouth to exist. To share. To LOVE.

Prison Number XR6890

lifeafterinprisonmentpsychiatrichosp.blogspot.co.uk

FRIDAY, 25 SEPTEMBER 2009

Trouble

Heathen Massive UK, Gospel Dance Music for Lesbian, Gay, Bisexual and Transgendered Supporter. Feel free to donate to www.aidsmap.com

Today I am in trouble again.

Why!?!

I have been trying to send cards and emails to Carolyn and I have been caught and my iPod touch and MacBook computer has been confiscated!

I retired to my bed and feel depressed and want to be referred to my group psychotherapy session. I am of the opinion that my peers will be able to help me to locate a cure for what ails me.

My psychiatrist mentioned that I may be experiencing the effects of the estrangement of my father, mother and son.

POSTED BY SAC WHO AT 11.10 NO COMMENTS

The Good, The Bad & The Ugly

Mother of my beloved bi... mixed heritaged son James... also of Jamaican Heritage... lived experiences of Psychi... Hospitalization due to a... SchizoAffective Disorder... Health diagnosis. I have Spent... in Her Majesty's Prison (HMP... Holloway Women's Prison) due to... Erotomania. I am an Atheist Christ... and supporter of Lesbian, Gay,... Bisexual & Transgendered. View m... work under...
YouTube

VIEW MY COMPLETE PROFILE

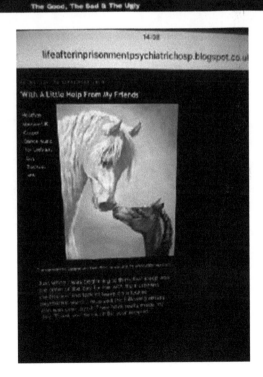

14.08

lifeafterinprisonmentpsychiatrichosp.blogspot.co.uk

"With A Little Help From My Friends"

RE: Peace One Day

From: hildegund Divine (hildegund39@hotmail.com)
Sent: 15 September 2009 07:29:38
To: yvonnepatriciastewart-williams@hotmail.co.uk

dearest Yvonne,

so pleased to hear to from you - of course I guessed that you
are in treatment, via Holloway though is a bit of a shock.
Good news is that you are able to contact me and I am
looking forward to seeing you soon, once this week is over
(the concert is in Paris this year !) Let me know how we can
meet and I'll be there........................

All the very best and lots of strength

Birgit

21

From: yvonnepatriciastewart-williams@hotmail.co.uk
To: hildegund39@hotmail.com
Subject: Peace One Day
Date: Mon, 14 Sep 2009 19:35:05 +0100

But not for you today.
Dear Birgit,

No prizes for guessing where I am?
Yes, Eileen Skellen Ward 3 of SLaM,
Maudsley Psychiatric Hospital
Denmark Hill. Via HMP Holloway.

What can I say, except Not this again.
And No, I have not seen James since
before his tenth birthday and no, I
don't know when I will be released.

Only today have I been able to find
your email on my phone as my old
account has closed and my battery
was flat. Please put this new email in
as my current.

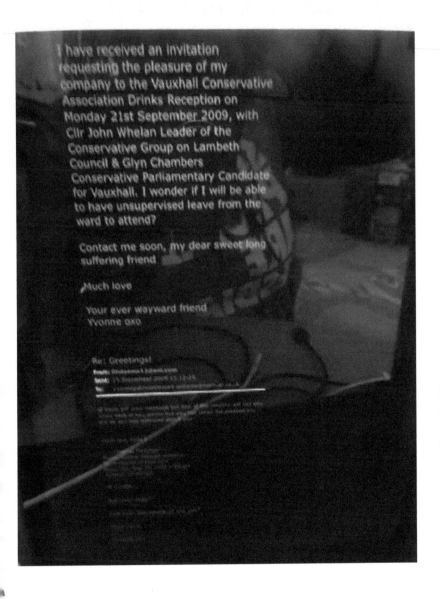

I have received an invitation requesting the pleasure of my company to the Vauxhall Conservative Association Drinks Reception on Monday 21st September 2009, with Cllr John Whelan Leader of the Conservative Group on Lambeth Council & Glyn Chambers Conservative Parliamentary Candidate for Vauxhall. I wonder if I will be able to have unsupervised leave from the ward to attend?

Contact me soon, my dear sweet long suffering friend

Much love

Your ever wayward friend
Yvonne oxo

Re: Greetings!

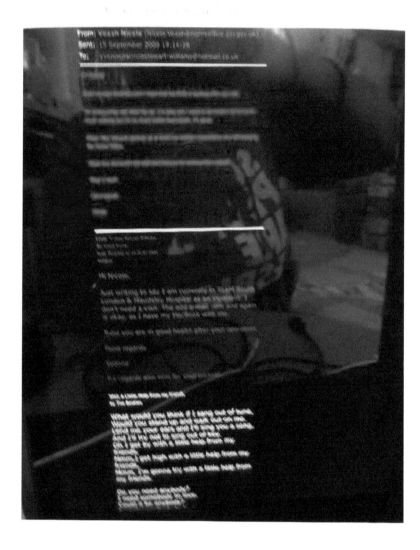

Prison Number XR6890

friends,
Mmm, I'm gonna try with a little help from
my friends.

Do you need anybody?
I need somebody to love.
Could it be anybody?
I want somebody to love.

What do I do when my love is away.
(Does it worry you to be alone)
How do I feel by the end of the day
(Are you sad because you're on your own)
No, I get by with a little help from my
friends,
Mmm, get high with a little help from my
friends,
Mmm, gonna to try with a little help from
my friends

Do you need anybody?
I need somebody to love.
Could it be anybody?
I want somebody to love.

Would you believe in a love at first sight?
Yes I'm certain that it happens all the time.
What do you see when you turn out the
light?
I can't tell you, but I know it's mine.
Oh, I get by with a little help from my
friends,
Mmm I get high with a little help from my
friends,
Oh, I'm gonna try with a little help from my
friends

Do you need anybody?
I just need someone to love.
Could it be anybody?
I want somebody to love

Oh, I get by with a little help from my
friends,
Mmm, gonna try with a little help from my
friends
Ooh, I get high with a little help from my
friends
Yes I get by with a little help from my
friends,
with a little help from my friends

TUESDAY, 15 SEPTEMBER 2009

Medication

Heathen Massive UK, Gospel Dance Music for Lesbian, Gay, Bisexual and Transgendered Supporter. Feel free to donate to

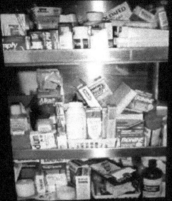

www.aidsmap.com

Yesterday I was allowed out of ES3 ward and out of SLaM psychiatric hospital accompanied by two people to visit my abode for a one off Section 17 leave. I was given a maximum of two hours, and amongst other things told that if I ran off, Carolyn Cowan HUGO would be contacted for the safety of her and her children and then the police would find me and I would be escorted back to HMP Holloway Women's Prison.

Last night, my trifluoperazine liquid anti-psychotic sugar-free oral medication was also increased from 25ml to 30mls. As a result, I am now sleeping almost every waking moment.

As a recovering addict, one day at a time, I find taking any kind of drugs including, alcohol and prescribed drugs challenging. Especially in the wake of the late Mr Michael Jackson, King of Pop. I am however added with this by reading the Sixth Edition of the Basic Text of Narcotics Anonymous which I received whilst in HMP Holloway Women Prison Supervised by RAPt.

Prison Number XR6890

lifeafterinprisonmentpsychiatrichosp.blogspot.co.uk

Some Ups, Some Downs

Heathen
Massive
UK,
Gospel
Dance
Music for
Lesbian,
Gay,
Bisexual
and

Transgendered Supporter. Feel free to donate to www.aidsmap.com

Oops. I've done it again.

to have unsupervised leave from the
ward to attend?

I won't keep you in suspense. The
answer my psychiatrist gave me was
NO.

www.glynforvauxhall.com/

POSTED BY YAC MIG AT 16:54 NO COMMENTS:

MONDAY, 14 SEPTEMBER 2009

Oops, I've done it again

Heathen Massive UK, Gospel Dance Music for Lesbian, Gay, Bisexual
and Transgendered Supporter. Feel free to donate to
www.aidsmap.com

Could bedwetting ever be viewed as cathartic?
Hmmm. Not by me. Today is the second time in
however many days, when the urine moisture has
past my nether regions and soiled my underwear
and mattress.

I suppose, when I think of fond memories of my
beloved son James aged five, with Carolyn Cowan
HUGO's beloved son Louis, I can smile again.
Louis had asked my son James, if he would like to
sleep over with him one night whilst we were at
Louis Parent's home after dining. My son said
without batting an eyelid that he wets his bed. That
did not deter the six year old Louis. Bless.

I think with this condition my sleepover days are at
an end.

This night, I beseeched a nurse to allow me the
priviledge of showering to wash the acidic urine off
my skin. The shower was cold and hardly flowing
with water anyway. I was interrupted before I had
properly dried myself...

It's all so self pitying...

I am alive, and I haven't been injured physically.
Any scars are of my own making. I have clean
bedding and a warm dry single locked room.

POSTED BY YAC MIG AT 04:28 NO COMMENTS:

Newer Posts   Home   Older Posts

Subscribe to: Posts (Atom)

14:11

lifeafterinprisonmentpsychiatrichosp.blogspot.co.uk

LIFE AFTER INPRISONMENT & PSYCHIATRIC HOSPITALS

SUNDAY, 13 SEPTEMBER 2009

'Keeping Up Appearances'

Quite

naturally, at this point in time, I am thinking about myself being safely ensconced at my rented Brixton abode. Just what will I say to Mr Anthony Hoggard [My long suffering neighbour] He is a professional actor and has been an absolute sweetie, a darling. How on earth am I to play my Hyointh role of 'Keeping Up Appearances' now that I have been publicly not just shaken but stirred! That mad- woman's been on the rampage again. This time via HMP Holloway womens prison. Loving a married woman with young children.

How can my beloved biological son James live out his school years and life, beyond bullying, with this legacy. My son James the university graduate, the international Airline Pilot ..Husband, father.

Yes, since his conception, I have given my beloved son James a steep hill to ascend, with many a boulder on his back to carry. How he will fare, one day at a time, only the Higher Power knows.

What I do know is, I love my son

Prison Number XR6890

lifeafterinprisonmentpsychiatrichosp.blogspot.co.uk

'UNder Pressure'

Heathen Massive UK, Gospel Dance Music for Lesbian, Gay, Bisexual and Transgendered Supporter. Feel free to donate to www.aidsmap.com

Gail Ann Dorsey is my earliest role models and love interest

I styled my hair like hers for years!

I didnt tell her that I had a serious love crush on her. Ok, I was certainly smitten with her. I just could find the words... but I truly meant and love her

Gail inadvertently resolved the problem... whilst doing some recording she introduced me to her HUSBAND!

here is Gail Ann Dorsey http://www.youtube.com/watc
h?v=wLDVGA-w1Es

I Wet My Bed

"I'LL SAY YOU SLEPT LIKE A BABY. YOU WET THE BED."

Heather: Healing UK, Gospel Dance Music for Lesbian, Gay, Bisexual and Transgendered Supporters. Feel free to donate to www.anderson.com

Last night, three nights into the increase of my trifluoperazine anti-psychotic liquid oral sugar-free medication to 25mls, I wet my bed at approximately 4:50 am today.

I confess that I have a genetically inherited bladder that signals that my bladder is full and requires emptying when it is half full. (This information was given to me via extensive test at Kings College GeneralHospital across the road from where I am now situated at SLaM Psychiatric Hospital).

My medication increase means that the signal is not picked up due to drowsiness caused by the mood / mind altering anti-psychotic medication. I have experienced this before on increased medication. My fluid intake is monitored via a meal / drinks word timetable. So I have not been drinking in excess and my medication suggests that alcohol is excluded whilst this medication is in use (I am in sobriety one day at a time, forever anyway). So there we have it. It is official. I am a bedwetter.

I have stripped from head to foot and placed myself in the shower. Used the last of my HMP Holloway canteen money purchased Dove soap and scrubbed myself. I have placed the clothes which have been wearing since 1st July 20.. in the washing machine and it is almost time to dry it. I am now dressed in a more expensive toddler and a toddler nightdress. Wiped headwear. Stiff and sodden have washed. Machine dryer on the ...

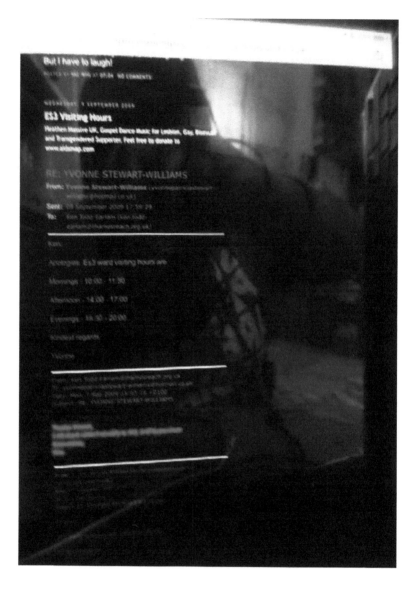

But I have to laugh!

WEDNESDAY, 9 SEPTEMBER 2009

ES3 Visiting Hours

Heathen Massive UK, Gospel Dance Music for Lesbian, Gay, Bisexual
and Transgendered Supporter. Feel free to donate to
www.aidsmap.com

RE: YVONNE STEWART-WILLIAMS

From: Yvonne Stewart-Williams (yvonnestewartwilliams@yahoo.co.uk)
Sent: 09 September 2009 17:14:24
To: Tom Todd Barton (tom.todd-barton@theresearch.org.uk)

Tom,

Apologies. Es3 ward visiting hours are

Mornings - 10:00 - 11:30

Afternoon - 14:00 - 17:00

Evenings - 16:30 - 20:00

Kindest regards,

Yvonne

lifeatterimprison____ __tpsychiatrichosp.blogspot.co.uk

PACE-Mental Health Advocacy

Heathen Massive UK, Gospel Dance Music for Lesbian, ___ _____
and Transgendered Supporter. Feel free to donate to ___
www.aidsmap.com

RE: Mental Health Advocacy needed asap!

From: Yvonne Stewart-Williams (yvonnepatricawilliams
williams@hotmail.co.uk)

Sent: 08 September 2009 14:18:47

To: advocacy@pace.earth.org.uk

Dear Ms Lewis,

Thank you for your prompt reply.

My housing issues are:

1) I am in rent arrears and on the brink of being evicted
for non payment of rent since 1st June 2009.

2) My council tax has not been paid since June 2009.

3) My Thames Water bill has not been paid since June
2009.

4) My electricity & gas bills have not been paid since June
2009.

5) My television licence has not been paid since June
2009.

I apologise. I am unable to complete your form online.

My borough is Lambeth.

Yours faithfully,

Yvonne Stewart-Williams(Ms)

Prison Number XR6890

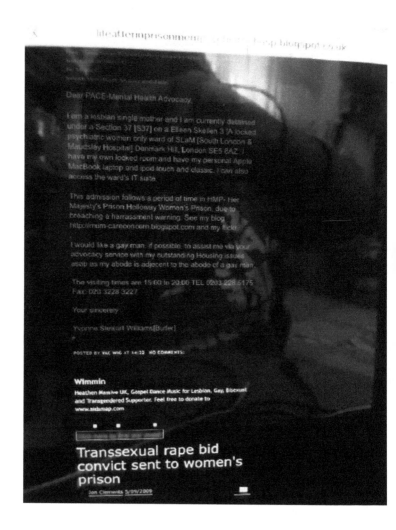

lifeafterimprisonment...blogspot.co.uk

Dear PACE-Mental Health Advocacy

I am a lesbian single mother and I am currently detained under a Section 37 [S37] on a Eileen Skellen 3 [A locked psychiatric woman only ward of SLaM [South London & Maudsley Hospital] Denmark Hill, London SE5 8AZ. I have my own locked room and have my personal Apple MacBook laptop and ipod touch and classic. I can also access the ward's IT suite.

This admission follows a period of time in HMP- Her Majesty's Prison Holloway Women's Prison, due to breaching a harrassment warning. See my blog http://mum-careconcern.blogspot.com and my flickr.

I would like a gay man, if possible, to assist me via your advocacy service with my outstanding Housing issues, asap as my abode is adjacent to the abode of a gay man.

The visiting times are 15:00 to 20:00 TEL 0203 228 5175 Fax: 020 3228 3227

Your sincerely

Yvonne Stewart Williams[Butler]

POSTED BY VAC WIG AT 14:22   NO COMMENTS:

Wimmin

Heathen Massive UK, Gospel Dance Music for Lesbian, Gay, Bisexual and Transgendered Supporter. Feel free to donate to www.aidsmap.com

Transsexual rape bid convict sent to women's prison

Jon Clements 5/09/2009

lifeafterinprisonmentpsychiatrichosp.blogspot.co.uk

LIFE AFTER INPRISONMENT & PSYCHIATRIC HOSPITALS

Eating / Sleeping well

Heathers Massive UK, Gospel Dance Music for Lesbian, Gay, Bisexual and Transgendered Supporter. Feel free to donate to www.aidsmap.com

Prison Number XR6890

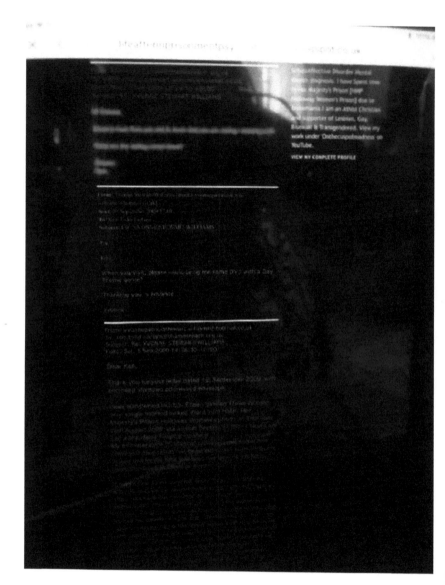

I AM LOVE

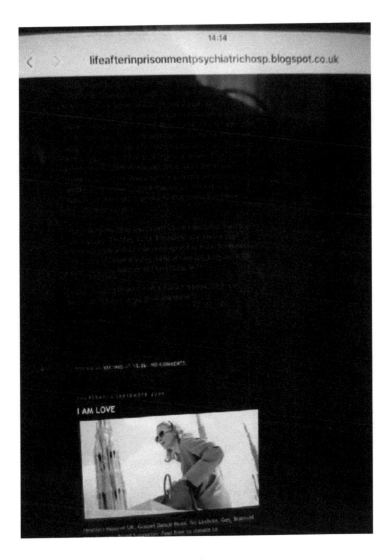

www.thamesreach.org.uk

Whatever happens, one day at a time, I am not shocked, I am www.gladd.co.uk/ **100% satisfied** with GLADD www.gladd.co.uk/

POSTED BY YAC MIG AT 12:55 NO COMMENTS:

WEDNESDAY, 2 SEPTEMBER 2009

Harry Potter

Heathen Massive UK, Gospel Dance Music for Lesbian, Gay, Bisexual and Transgendered Supporter. Feel free to donate to www.aidsmap.com

Just returned to my room, after unsuccessfully trying to watch the Harry Potter 'Goblet of Fire' film on terrestrial television in the communal lounge of this locked psychiatric women only ward. Harry Potter books and movies are one of my favourites. I have watched every one at the cinema, except this one. I have all the books except the latest. And all the films except this one. When I was last in Edinburgh, I passed a place which was said to be Ms JK Rowlings choice to frequent as a writer. Once ensconced back at my full time employment I shall purchased these.

I bought my son a Harry Potter toothbrush, when he was younger and other such gifts. I have given him his own movies and books of Harry Potter, and am delighted when I am able to watch and read them with him.

Fortunately I have been able to use my Apple MacBook laptop to access my e-mails, and was pleasantly surprised to receive the following:

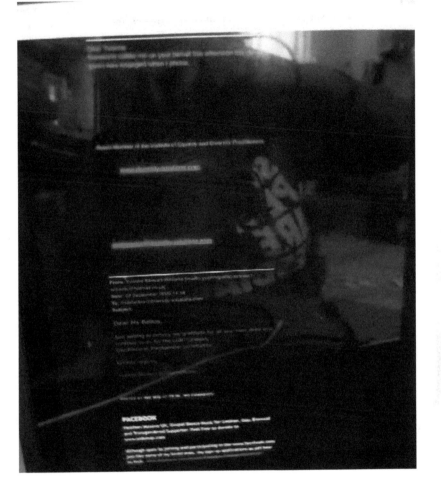

FACEBOOK

Heathen Massive UK, Gospel Dance Music for Lesbian, Gay, Bisexual and Transgendered Supporter. Feel free to donate to www.aidsmap.com

Although open to joining and participating in the www.facebook.com just like some of my loved ones, my sign up applications as yet bear no fruit. www.facebook.com/pages/Carolyn-Cowan/0000

POSTED BY YAC WIG AT 11:21 NO COMMENTS:

THANK YOU

Heathen Massive UK, Gospel Dance Music for Lesbian, Gay, Bisexual and Transgendered Supporter. Feel free to donate to www.aidsmap.com

Thank you for my personal copy of the Sixth Edition, which I received whilst in HMP Holloway Women's Prison within the first few days of my incrisonment. WWW.na.org

POSTED BY YAC WIG AT 10:00 NO COMMENTS:

TUESDAY, 1 SEPTEMBER 2009

My nickname is just 'YAC wig'

Heathen Massive UK, Gospel Dance Music for Lesbian, Gay, Bisexual and Transgendered Supporter. Feel free to donate to www.aidsmap.com

Heathen Massive UK, Gospel Dance Music for Lesbian, Gay, Bisexual and Transgendered Supporter is at My biological mother's home of several decades is in Luton, Bedfordshire. Her home is the Headquarters of Heathen Massive UK. She is a Jehovah's Witness of many years and good standing. You may address her as Sister Brown although her secular title is Mrs Lillan A. Brown. Italian with a 'L.'Feel free to donate to www.aidsmap.com

In this imovie I give an explanation of my nickname. I posted it on my YouTube 'Onthecuspofmadness' site yesterday. Enjoy.

One more thing. Today my psychiatrist told me that my trifluoperazine (stelazine) oral liquid sugar free anti-psychotic medication is to be increased from 6mls to 15mls this evening. I am Not surprised buy this decision. I am on a locked ward in a psychiatric hospital to be cured of my showing my love for a woman that I love.

I don't care. It won't interfere with my love of Carolyn Cowan HUGO, one day at a time, into and beyond infinity... I love the beautiful 'I AM LOVE' theme. Once I return to my full time employment I shall purchase the 'I AM LOVED' for myself and my loved ones from the same www.devotion.co.uk online retailer.

Prison Number XR6890

LIFE AFTER INPRISONMENT & PSYCHIATRIC HOSPITALS

TUESDAY, 1 SEPTEMBER 2009

PRISON NUMBER: XR6890

Heathen Massive UK, Gospel Dance Music for Lesbian, Gay, Bisexual and Transgendered Supporter. Feel free to donate to www.sickmap.com

My Her Majesty's Prison [HMP] Holloway number was XR6890. During my time as a prisoner in HMP Holloway Women's Prison in Islington, London UK, I visited the Library in the Education department, during free flow. Whilst in the Education department on the 14th July 2009, I took part in a creative writing session and wrote the testimony contained in this imovie, which I film today Tuesday 1st September 2009, here on [ES3] 'Eileen Skellen Three'. The locked women only [SLaM] South London & Maudsley Psychiatric Hospital ward in Camberwell, London UK. I presented the written testimony for publication in 'SHUT...UP' UK Prisoners magazine. I will now attempt to upload this testimony imovie. Whilst waiting I am listening to some of my Gospel & Religious dance music which I have on my ipod. I am indeed truly fortunate to have been present in HMP Holloway Women's Prison for and took part in the [CofE] Church of England's as well as the [RC] Roman Catholic's Holy Communion. I feel a bit like Ex-Offender; Nelson Mandela.

Prison Number XR6890

MONDAY 11 AUGUST 2009

One Year to the day...

Heathen Massive UK, Gospel Dance Music for Lesbian, Gay, Bisexual and Transgendered Supporter. Feel free to donate to www.aidsmap.com

Today marks one year to the day since I have had the pleasure of utilizing www.blogger.com I started with my 'On the Cusp of Madness' blog then 'Care & Concern' blog and since my release from HMP Holloway, I have been writing this blog. Yesterday I uploaded a couple of imovies which I have made whilst I am in SLaM psychiatric hospital, on an acute locked women's ward on 'Youtube'. I shall attempt to upload them both for you. Together they are approximately four minutes in duration. I added another imovie today, but that is almost ten minutes.

Tomorrow is September and then it's Black History month, World Mental Health Day, as well as both my and Lady Margaret Thatcher's shared birthday. I am looking forward to returning to, my meetings, my full-time employment, my abode, paying my bills, contact with my beloved son, and my mother, as well as, actively campaigning for my Conservative Political Party in Brixton...

Prison Number XR6890

<

SUNDAY, 11 AUGUST 2009

I LOVE her

I LOVE her
[Carloyn Cowan HUGO]
Heathen Massive UK, Gospel Dance Music for Lesbian, Gay, Bisexual
and Transgendered Supporter. Feel free to donate to
https://www.aidsmap.com/

I have now been safely ensconced on the locked psychiatric Eileen
Skellen 3 (ES3) Women's ward of the South London Maudsley Hospital
[SLaM] for ten days. I arrived here from A4 wing of HMP Holloway
womens Prison on Thursday 20th August 2009, on a court section
937. The Judge of South Western Magistrate court followed the advice
of my court psychiatric report and probation.
So What!
I said I was guilty from the very start.

I have been recording podcasts on my personal 'apple macbook' and
listening to and viewing my ipod touch and classic. I have made a few
personal short movies, one for my beloved son James, Carolyn Cowan
HUGO [I Love her] and of myself.

I am currently situated in the aferis IT suite on ES3 and have just been
handed the correspondence of a routledge Taylor & Francis Group
www.routledge.com/history catalogue. I am awaiting with Routledge as I
purchased the 'Whole who of Lesbian and Gay history by Wotherspoon
and Aldrich Vol 1 & Vol 2 from this publisher and gained the autograph
of the Bishop Rev Gene Robinson

Yesterday's the Guardian Newspaper had an article about Rev Gene
Robinson

Trifluoperazine sugar free liquid drops is administered to me each night.
Since 2nd July 2009, I have remained on unpaid leave from my full
time paid employment with Thames Reach Bondage.

During my time in HMP Holloway I wrote a 'Bent...Straight' piece for the
Bent... Mr 124 Prison magazine, I am of few moderators that it may
have been published.

lifeafterinprisonmentpsychiatrichosp.blogspot.co.uk

'Shut... Up' UK Prison magazine, I am of the impression that I may have been published.

Rough Justice? No way! I love that woman and her children Louis & Isadora.

POSTED BY 18C NIG at 11:31 NO COMMENTS

Rear View Mirror

This is what a loving couple looks like

Rear View Mirror

My theory. A tribute to Heterosexual Monogamous Loving Trusting Respectful, supportive couples.

The reciprocated loving Sexual Coitus of a woman to her male husband of penetrative anal stimulation , with the use of a dildo [strapped on or otherwise] purchased a outlets such as 'Ann Summers' example Old Compton Street SOHO, London W1 [West One] UK

Open mindedness, willingness and honesty are essential requirements.

This theory is an idea[ist to my, with 'Land is Live' theory which can be found on my other [or the Case of Machine, at LiveCoroner page

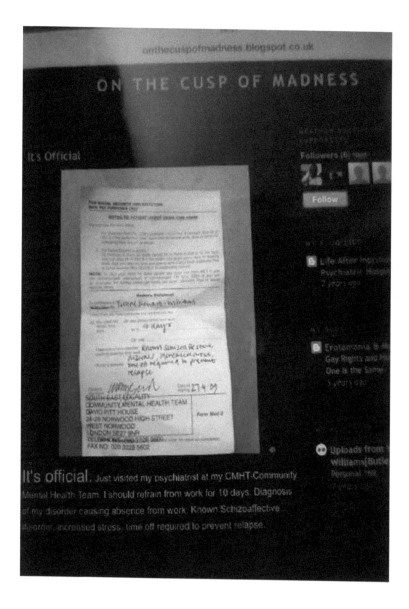

onthecuspofmadness.blogspot.co.uk

ON THE CUSP OF MADNESS

It's Official

Followers (6)

Follow

It's official. Just visited my psychiatrist at my CMHT-Community Mental Health Team. I should refrain from work for 10 days. Diagnosis of my disorder causing absence from work: Known Schizoaffective disorder, increased stress, time off required to prevent relapse.

Prison Number XR6890

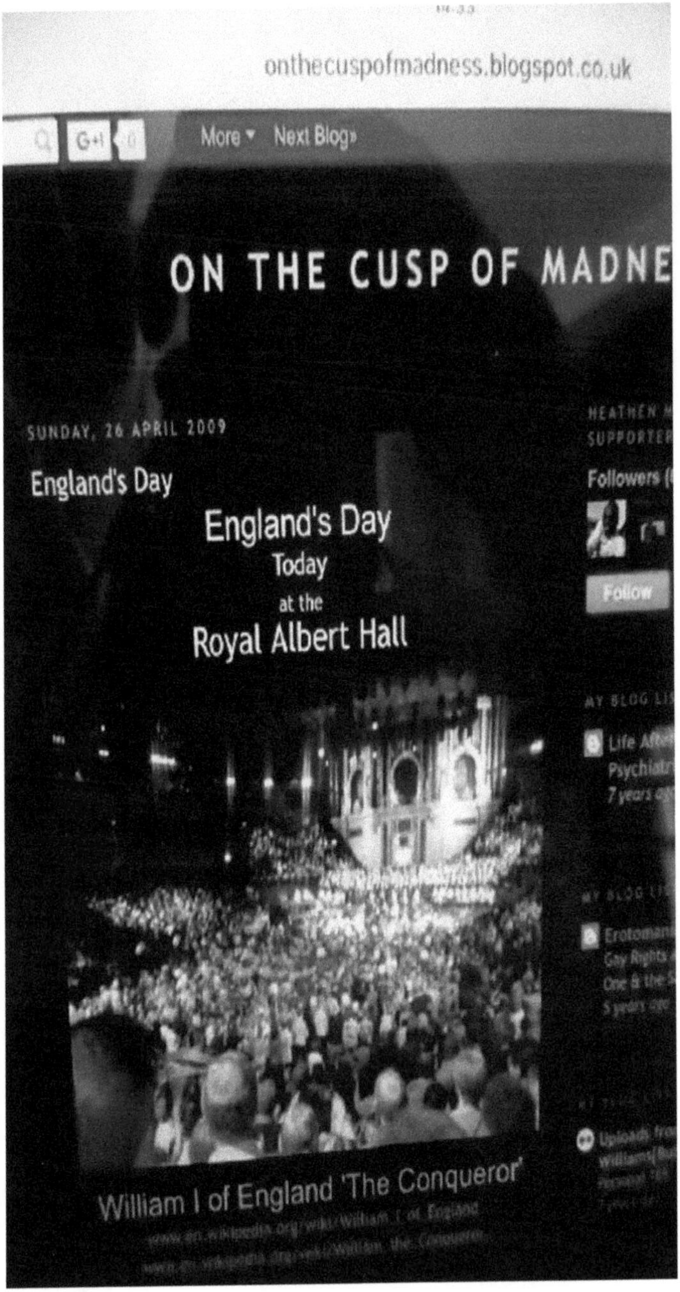

Prison Number XR6890

SATURDAY, 25 APRIL 2009

The Perfect Storm

I was late leaving work this evening, and, as a result ended up being half an hour late calling my beloved son. I am broke, and have absolutely no idea what I am going to do with my son next week during our five and a half hours together. I would have loved to have taken him to revisit the Bank of England Museum www.bankofengland.co.uk/education/museum I first took him to visit it while he was living with me, but if my memory serves me correctly it doesn't open on Saturdays.

It was truly a joy to converse with my son - nothing new about that, or the fact that I was filled with gratitude. He is a 'Gift' and a 'Miracle'. I feel so blessed, to be able to lavishly and overtly, convey my love and affections for my son to him and for it to be requited - just as from my mother to me.

Yesterday my mother rang me again. I know that she is concerned about me at this time, as she yet again told me to come to her, reminding me that I will always have a home with her. I have been cautiously negotiating with my own personal 'stress abyss' quick sand. I know excessive residence means certain spiritual death.

I just can't afford to be so self absorb and self pitying to take for granted the fact that I do have some contact with my child. Heartbreakingly, for what ever the reason, many equally sincerely loving parents and guardians are unable.

I am 'On Call' tonight and one of my client who knew I was 'On Call' has just rung me and asked me to watch 'The Perfect Storm' on Channel 7. 'God works in mysterious ways He wonders He performs'

***

Two days ago, I received an invitation from Ed Watkins, Deputy Chairman of Dulwich and West Norwood Conservative Association, to attend a forthcoming new members drinks evening. The long and the short of it is, I declined the invitation and requested to be invited to attend a coffee morning. All credit to him, today I received a coffee invite offer at some point.

is will be at 1.45 to allow time in case
on event will begin at 2.30 prompt and
where you will be invited to attend the 2
Street to carry on the day, there will be a
in with light refreshments.

of Rendell Close, for those coming by
er ground station is Clapham Junction
es that leave from the rear or the side of

d rank outside the Junction for those
t...

---

st, but not least:

work today, I found that I had received my
Clapton with special guests ARC
Hall at 7:30pm on Thursday, 28th May 2009.

Inspirational

ve, I will make a start on reading

Eric Clapton

Autobiography

on.co.uk/Eric-Clapton-
aphy/dp/1846051606

T-WILLIAMS(BUTLER) AT 19:32

'Big Momma's House'
Education For All Conference
Hand in Hand
Happy St. George's Day
Fraught
Edinburgh
Surrey County Cricket Club
    battingtoday at The Ov...
For Your Information
Clarissa Dickson Wright
Revitalised by Vitalise
Awake!
Happy Easter!!
Anybody See My Trial?
ALDO BUSI
Attitude
Grace Returns
Gifts
God Is Spirit
Yes, Jesus Loves Me
99% APR
GOD
Silvio Berlusconi
I Am With French Friends
'Love It!'
Concorde
'Faith Without Works Is Dead'

► March (41)
► February (26)
► January (17)

► 2008 (159)

Prison Number XR6890

Yvonne Stewart-Will
@yvonne_S_W
I aim to be the First Black Openly Lesbian Conservative Member of
Parliament to take a seat at the 2020 General Election.

📍 London UK 🔗 mini-career.com/ngs0001.co.uk
📅 Born on 13 October 1961

252 FOLLOWING   200 FOLLOWERS

TWEETS   TWEETS & REPLIES   MEDIA   LIKES

Yvonne Stewart-Will @yvonne_S_W 10/10/2016
Please text me your support on: +44 7490 165136. Please
also Look at and forward my link: gofundme.com/xue7207u

Yvonne Stewart-Will @Yvonne_S_W 04/04/2017

Yvonne Stewart-Will @Yvonne_S_W 02/04/2017
Police Lives Matters youtube.com/watch?v=koYBAg...

Yvonne Stewart-Will @Yvonne_S_W 06/04/2017
Police Lives Matters youtu.be/koYBAg10VeM?a via
@YouTube

Yvonne Stewart-Will @yvonne_S_W 03/04/2017

Prison Number XR6890

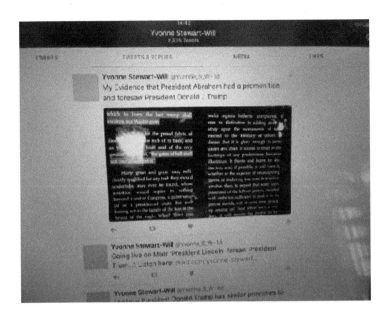

Yvonne Stewart-Will @yvonne_S_W · 1d
My Evidence that President Abraham had a premonition and foresaw President Donald . Trump

Yvonne Stewart-Will @yvonne_S_W · 1d
Going live on Mixlr 'President Lincoln foresaw President Trump ... Listen here: mixlr.com/yvonne-stewart...

Yvonne Stewart-Will @yvonne_S_W · 1d
I believe President Donald Trump has similar priorities to

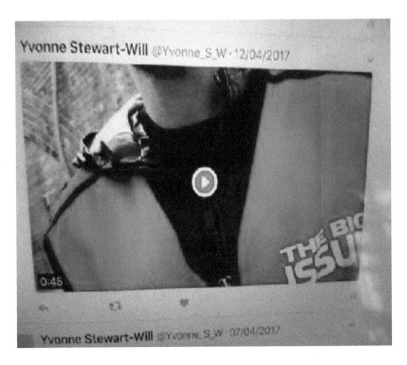

Yvonne Stewart-Will @Yvonne_S_W · 12/04/2017

THE BIG ISSUE

0:45

Yvonne Stewart-Will @Yvonne_S_W · 07/04/2017

Prison Number XR6890

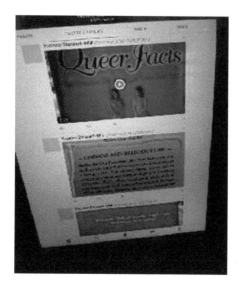

Prison Number XR6890

Queer Facts

Yvonne Stewart-Will @Yvonne_S_W 26/03/2017

2 Years Ago

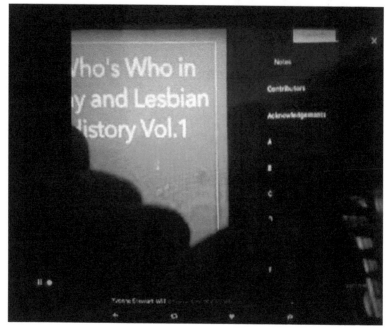

Prison Number XR6890

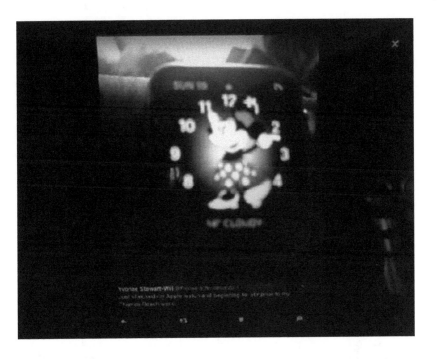

It was a privilege to have both Julian my long term lover and James my son beside me wholeheartedly participating in this event in

Yvonne Stewart-Will @Yvonne_S_W_ 11/08/2017

Prison Number XR6890

Yvonne Stewart-Will @Yvonne_N_Will · Nov 2012
got my Stonewall laces in my Clarks. Gone tax footwear

Prison Number XR6890

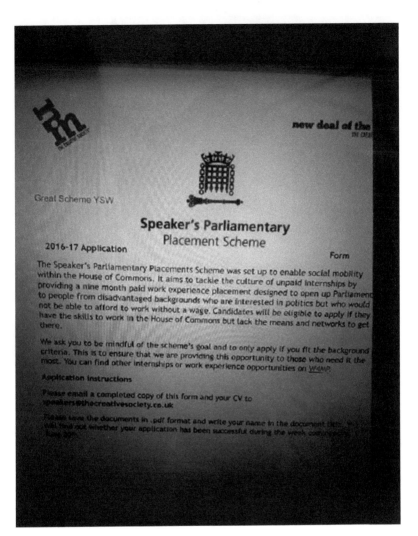

new deal of the

Great Scheme YSW

Speaker's Parliamentary
Placement Scheme

2016-17 Application

Form

The Speaker's Parliamentary Placements Scheme was set up to enable social mobility within the House of Commons. It aims to tackle the culture of unpaid internships by providing a nine month paid work experience placement designed to open up Parliament to people from disadvantaged backgrounds who are interested in politics but who would not be able to afford to work without a wage. Candidates will be eligible to apply if they have the skills to work in the House of Commons but lack the means and networks to get there.

We ask you to be mindful of the scheme's goal and to only apply if you fit the background criteria. This is to ensure that we are providing this opportunity to those who need it the most. You can find other internships or work experience opportunities on W4MP.

Application instructions

Please email a completed copy of this form and your CV to
speakers@thecreativesociety.co.uk

Please save the documents in .pdf format and write your name in the document title. You will find out whether your application has been successful during the week commencing June 20.

Still On The
Cusp Of Madness
One Day At A Time
Ten Years On

By Yvonne Stewart-Williams

chimpwithmokapublishing
the mental health publisher

Prison Number XR6890

🕐 3 Years

🔒 Only you can see this unless you share it

➤ Share

See More Memories ›

Stewart-Will @Yvonne_S.W · 25/02/2017

Prison Number XR6890

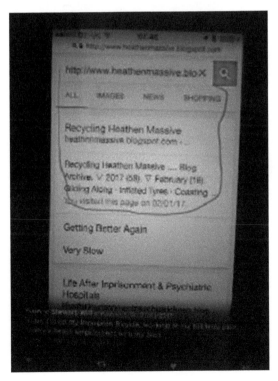

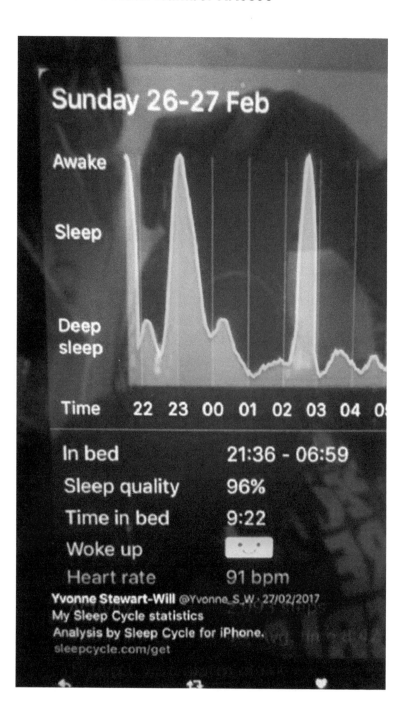

Sunday 26-27 Feb

Awake

Sleep

Deep
sleep

Time   22 23 00 01 02 03 04 0

In bed	21:36 - 06:59
Sleep quality	96%
Time in bed	9:22
Woke up	🙂
Heart rate	91 bpm

Yvonne Stewart-Will @Yvonne_S_W · 27/02/2017
My Sleep Cycle statistics
Analysis by Sleep Cycle for iPhone.
sleepcycle.com/get

Prison Number XR6890

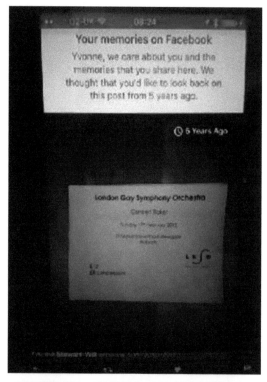

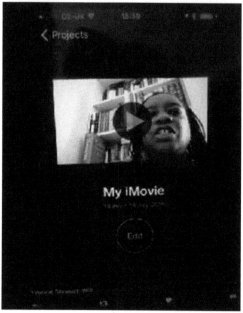

Prison Number XR6890

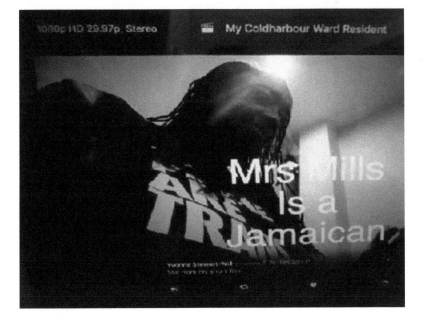

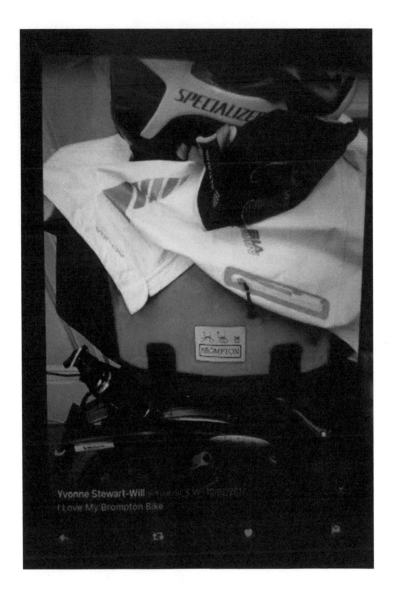

Prison Number XR6890

Yvonne Stewart-Will @Yvonne_S_W 09/02/2017
Me today at my paid Thames Reach Waterloo Project employment

Yvonne Stewart-Will @Yvonne_S_W · 28/01/2017
Me, earlier today at CCHQ - Conservative Central Headquarters

Yvonne Stewart-Will @Yvonne_S_W · 23/01/2017
Me, earlier today next to Margaret Thatcher's image in the Board
room of CCHQ with the CWO

Prison Number XR6890

Yvonne Stewart-Will @Yvonne SW 21/06/2018
Me just now with cabinet minister Margot James MP at our
LGBT/QRY event

Yvonne Stewart-Will @Yvonne SW 21/06/2018
Mental Health Event in the House of Lords

Prison Number XR6890

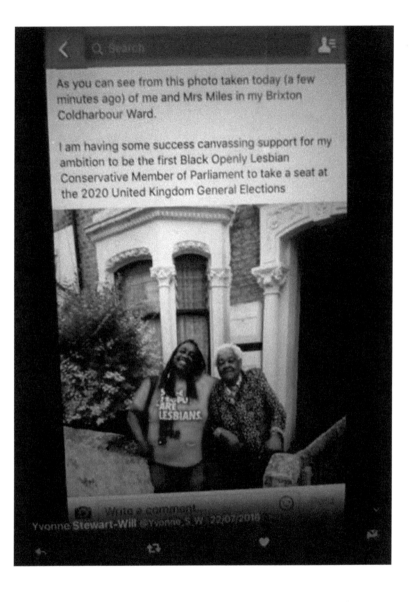

As you can see from this photo taken today (a few minutes ago) of me and Mrs Miles in my Brixton Coldharbour Ward.

I am having some success canvassing support for my ambition to be the first Black Openly Lesbian Conservative Member of Parliament to take a seat at the 2020 United Kingdom General Elections

Yvonne Stewart-Will @Yvonne_S_W 22/07/2016

Prison Number XR6890

Yvonne Stewart-Will @Yvonne_S_W 15/07/2015
Day off Today, spending quality time having lunch & walking in the
park with my dear friend Laura. #WorkLifeBalance

Yvonne Stewart-Will @Yvonne_S_W · 14/07/2016
me with A few London Metropolitan police officers.

This photo was taken today by one of my homeless hostel clients.

Yvonne Stewart-Wil @Yvonne.S.W 26/06/2016
Socialising at Black Pride

Yvonne Stewart Williams Butler and LGBTory
shared LGBTory's photo.

LGBTory
1 hr · 🌍

Ready for Pride in London. MG

Prison Number XR6890

Yvonne Stewart-Will @Yvonne_S_W · 15/02/2016
Just been for a drink of bottled sparkling water with lemon and lime slices at my local Brixton Coldharbour Ward...

Prison Number XR6890

Yvonne Stewart-Will...
...at Winter Church Remembered

Yvonne Stewart-Will...
Me wearing a Stonewall Trans T-shirt with Lord Michael Cashman on my left and Rev Sharon Ferguson on my right

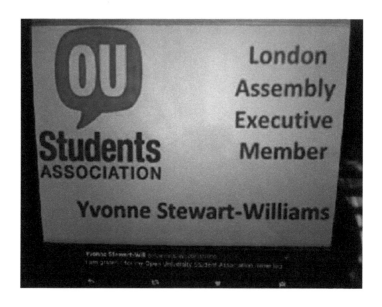

Prison Number XR6890

Yvonne Stewart-Will @Yvonne_S_W 10/01/2016
I am grateful for my first visit to Brighton as a lesbian with my
mother (see photo)and then my first visit to...

Yvonne Stewart-Will @Yvonne_S_W 10/01/2016
...Brighton Pride with my beloved son James (see photo) and my
first Duties in Brighton at my...

Prison Number XR6890

Prison Number XR6890

Prison Number XR6890

Prison Number XR6890

Grateful. This is a photo of the Effra Hall pub on Rattray Road, Brixton, Coldharbour Ward.

Prison Number XR6890

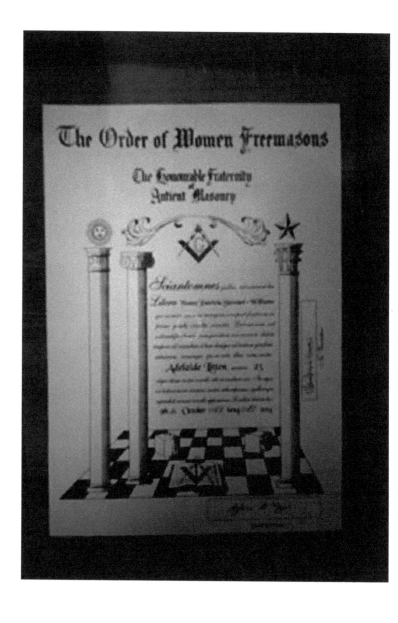

Prison Number XR6890

Prison Number XR6890

Prison Number XR6890

Prison Number XR6890

ON THE CUSP OF MADNESS

Mental Health Media Awards 2008.
www.open-up.org.uk

Me & John Bird

Prison Number XR6890

Prison Number XR6890

Prize Giving Day Ceremony 2013/2014

Prison Number XR6890

Prison Number XR6890

Prison Number XR6890

CPSIA information can be obtained
at www.ICGtesting.com
Printed in the USA
LVHW071806210922
728950LV00018B/228/J

9 781783 826421